TRACES

ROLL C

For John Peel.
An old cricketer who left the crease far
too soon, his show provided inspiration for
my writing and for Jade's music.
Jade would have adored him.

KINGFISHER
An imprint of Kingfisher Publications Plc
New Penderel House, 283-288 High Holborn
London WC1V 7HZ
www.kingfisherpub.com

This edition published by Kingfisher 2007
First published by Kingfisher 2005
2 4 6 8 10 9 7 5 3 1

Text copyright © Malcolm Rose 2005

A CIP catalogue record for this book
is available from the British Library.

ISBN 978 0 7534 1495 8

Printed in India
1TR/0307/THOM/(THOM)/80TORA/C

TRACES

ROLL CALL

MALCOLM ROSE

KINGFISHER

ABOUT THE AUTHOR

Malcolm Rose, a former Senior Lecturer in Chemistry, is a well-known children's thriller writer of some 25 novels including five *Traces* titles. Malcolm has won the Angus Book Award and the Lancashire Book of the Year Award. His books regularly feature in the Book Trust 100 best books for children list. In the USA, *Traces: Framed!* was selected as a Best International Book by the International Reading Association. Malcolm lives in Sheffield.

Chapter One

Emily Wonder's eyes did not narrow when the dazzling sunshine fell across her face. Her numbed eyelids did not snap shut to protect her from the blinding light. Lying across the sofa, she was helpless against the unbearable smarting pain in her eyes. Tears and sweat rolled down her cheeks into the soft cushion. She was not tied to the settee but she was completely unable to shift her position. However much she tried, she could not move an arm, a leg, her head or any other part of her body. She could not even blink an eyelid. She just lay there in her apartment, tethered by invisible bonds, as if immobilized by an overwhelming weight, and waited to die.

It had been a good day until, feeling faint, she'd lain down on the sofa after lunch and become limp within minutes. First, she'd felt a prickling around her mouth. The tingling had spread pleasantly throughout her body, bringing a feeling of lazy warmth. But then came the shivering, the agonizing pins and needles in her fingertips, tongue and nose, and the waves of nausea as her ailing nervous system shut down. Her mind remained agonizingly clear, though, as she realized that she was not suffering merely from heat exhaustion.

* * *

In this extraordinarily hot summer, the weather was striving to turn the country into a desert. Reservoirs were running dry and rivers were reduced to sad trickles. On the day of Emily's death, Dundee sweltered. The ski centre's exhausted air-conditioning system took its last breath and broke down. The indoor slope defrosted immediately and the snow melted away. The Music Hall, Caird Theatre, and the McManus Art Gallery were packed with people seeking leisure and an escape from the heat.

Along Riverside Walkway the tarmac was sticky underfoot. In the morning, Emily hesitated as she strolled past the beautifully preserved sailing ships moored in the docks. For a few minutes, she gazed at cabs speeding over the wide estuary on the impressive Tay Bridge. The iron railings divided the sunlight so that the cabs seemed to move under strobe lighting. It made their crossing appear jerky rather than smooth.

Just as she was about to continue her walk, an older woman bumped into her and muttered, "Oops. Sorry."

Emily shrugged. "That's okay." Even wearing sunglasses, she had to squint in the sunlight to get a good view of the person who had nudged her. But the woman had pulled a wide-brimmed hat down protectively over her eyes. Half of her face was in shadow. Emily watched her walk slowly away. She was dressed in a short skirt and flimsy floral top. With every step, she placed one foot deliberately right in front of the other, giving her the flamboyant bearing of a fashion model.

Carrying on along Riverside Walk, Emily visited Dundee Animal Sanctuary. There, the vets were making garlic ice cream for the animals to keep them cool. For the first time, the amphibian house did not need power to maintain its tropical conditions. The yellow-splashed Californian newts and harlequin frogs were lapping up the sunshine. The aquarium and sea-life tanks had to be cooled to keep the water hospitable for the pufferfish, the tiny blue-ringed octopus, the garish angelfish and xanthid crabs.

Emily took lunch in the conservation park's restaurant. When she presented her identity card, the attendant asked a question that Emily had suffered a hundred times.

"Are you *the* Emily Wonder?"

Shaking her head and smiling, Emily pulled down her sunglasses and gave her usual response. "If I started to sing, you'd know right away I'm not. I share a name with her, not a voice."

"Shame."

Keen to end the stale conversation, Emily visited the washroom and then returned to tuck into the fish and salad.

Afterwards, thinking that the heat was taking its toll on her, she got up to go straight home. Just as she got to the door, though, someone called her name. She turned to see a man dashing up to her.

He was shorter than Emily, but older. He had a big bushy beard and, even indoors, he was wearing a cap. Under its peak, his eyes were intense. His left arm was encased in plaster and hooked across his chest.

She had never seen him before in her life. Startled, Emily stepped back and her bare arm touched one of the cacti on a shelf. The plant's sharp spines pierced her skin. "Ouch!"

The man glanced at the large flat cactus with clumps of brown spines and then looked into Emily's face. "You're all right. Just a sting. It's not poisonous."

Rubbing the spot where the prickles had scratched her, she said, "What do you want? How do you know my name?"

The strange man held out her identity card in his right palm. "You left it on the table."

"Oh. Silly me. Thank you," she replied, taking it from him. Feeling light-headed, she opened the door and made for her apartment.

The sun executed an arc high in the clear sky and the vertical blinds in Emily's window chopped the harsh light into bands of shade and brilliance, turning her living room into a cage with dark bars that drifted throughout the afternoon. Emily could have counted the hours by the alternate periods of welcome shade and tortuous glare on her inert face. So much perspiration cascaded from her body that she felt as if she'd just walked through a rainstorm. Her muscles were paralysed but her brain was fully aware that she was about to die from inevitable heart failure or suffocation. Robbed of speech and motion, there was nothing she could do about it. She was defenceless against the unknown and unseen poison that had penetrated every part of her body except her mind. Cruelly, the chemical could not cross into her brain, so she remained perfectly conscious.

For seven hours, Emily experienced her young life slipping slowly away. For seven hours, she was a zombie – alive and awake, yet to all intents and purposes, lifeless.

She was aware of time passing and the pain of her organs failing one by one, but she was not aware that she had been murdered.

The forensic investigator assigned to Emily's death did not realize that she had been murdered either. A thorough examination of her body did not reveal any evidence of a crime. Even the pathologist who conducted the post-mortem did not find the true cause of death. The toxicity tests on her blood were negative.

The microscopic puncture wounds and inflammation on her left forearm were trivial, caused by the tiny spines of a prickly-pear cactus, *Opuntia vulgaris*. All of her internal organs had been healthy when they had suddenly ceased to function. The pathologist put her death down to heart failure as a result of unknown natural causes.

Without a trace of unlawful killing, The Authorities closed the case.

Chapter Two

A crazy year was coming to an end. The summer had been the hottest and driest on record. In October, Luke Harding had graduated from Birmingham School as a Forensic Investigator at the age of sixteen. Autumn rains had come late but, when they did, they made November the wettest in memory. Now, on Sunday the 25th of December, an unusually severe winter had got a grip on the country.

Every roof had turned startlingly white with frost. Every windowpane had become opaque with stringy spiders' webs stretching across the frames. The overgrown grass in the parks was silvery like the greying hair of an old man. Thirsty birds looked in frustration at frozen ponds. The lake beside Woburn Wood was solid and, through the trees, Luke could hear the excited cries of skaters. The hillside opposite was thick with snow and toboggans. At the bottom of the gentle slope, children were engaged in a snowball battle. Some were probably not much younger than Luke. But Luke was dealing with something altogether more adult and serious. His role as a FI separated him from the other kids and separated him from fun.

The leafless trees had suspended their life until spring. In the brook, a little cold water trickled under what seemed to be a plate of glass. The banks were lined with great clumps of ice and, above it, long smooth icicles hung down from the branches. Only the holly and the victim's clothing added colour to the black-and-white world of the wood.

Luke was keeping well back from the young woman's body while his Mobile Aid to Law and Crime scanned and recorded the scene. "Any footprints?" he asked Malc, his breath coming out of his mouth like smoke.

"No," the robot answered. "Fresh snowfall has covered any tracks."

"So, there could be something interesting under the top layer."

"My scan penetrates snow. I have not detected any significant evidence within ten metres."

"All right." Stepping carefully on the white surface, Luke walked up to the victim who was lying flat on her back. He crouched down near her bloodless and goose-pimply face. In death, she looked older than her age. She was probably eighteen to twenty-five years old. Her hair seemed to be standing on end, as if she'd been scared witless in the moment that she died. But Luke knew that the goose pimples and the state of her hair had nothing to do with cold or shock. Rigor mortis had stiffened the tiny muscles around each follicle, making her hair stand out and dotting her flesh. He glanced down at her chest where her clothing was torn and matted with the brown stain of congealed blood. There was no sign of the weapon that had ended her life. "What caused the wound, Malc? A knife?"

"No. Its cross-section is round, not narrow."

"Something like a screwdriver, then?" Thinking of the woodland surroundings, he added, "Or a sharp stick?"

Malc was hovering on the other side of the young woman's body. "I cannot rule out a screwdriver but the weapon was not wooden. It is a clean wound. I do not detect any bacteria, infection, or residue of any sort."

Luke felt sickened. She was still a girl really, only a few years older than himself, and possibly too young to have been paired with a husband. Trying to swallow his disgust, he said with a dark smile, "I've been watching too many horror films. A stake through the heart would leave tiny splinters or dirt behind. If this is just a clean hole, it's like she was stabbed by thin air."

"It is not possible…"

Luke put up his hand. "Don't tell me. I know. Air can't be thin and you can't stab anyone with it." He inched his way around the body looking carefully for anything interesting. His hands were aching from the cold and his fingers began to feel numb.

The victim was dressed for the weather. She was wearing a fleece coat and several layers underneath. Around her neck was a distinctive yellow scarf. "Perhaps the pathologist will see something after getting all these clothes off."

"That is possible but I have conducted a microscopic scan in the area of the wound."

"There's something else that's strange. I'm not convinced this is a fatal wound. It's gone in on the right side of her chest, missing the heart."

"Correct, but there was massive blood loss."

"Mmm. What's your best guess at the time of death?"

"I do not guess," Malc replied. "I estimate. The body is cold and rigor mortis is fully established. Death occurred one to two days ago."

"Scan her eyes, please. They look different to me."

"There is a contact lens in her left eye."

"Not in the right?"

"Correct."

"Okay. Let's get her details." Luke knelt down, pulled on latex gloves and removed the girl's identity card from her shoulder bag. "Emily Wonder. Aged eighteen." It took him a few seconds to call the name to mind and then he muttered, "She's a food technologist so she can't be *the* Emily Wonder. Not the opera singer. Anyway, access her medical records, Malc, and check her eyesight. Was her right eye normal?"

"Searching."

While he waited, Luke asked, "You've got the details of whoever found her?"

"Confirmed. It was a male walker. He claimed to be going through the wood to join the ice-skating."

Luke stood upright and sighed. To the south, an imposing building was perched grimly on the rise. "Has anyone escaped from Woburn Prison?"

"I do not have that information. I will request it." Malc paused and then announced, "The victim was shortsighted to the same extent in both eyes."

"So, we've got a missing contact lens. Ultraviolet scan of the area, Malc. See if you can find it."

The white snow glowed brighter, and slightly blue, under Malc as he swept a beam of ultraviolet light over the floor of the wood. Finishing the scan, he concluded, "It is not in the immediate vicinity."

"Interesting. Have any similar deaths been reported?"

"Searching."

Low-level movement on Luke's left caught his eye and at once he spun round. But it was only a fox. The animal was probably curious about the smell of death among the gaunt trees. Seeing Luke, it slunk away in the opposite direction. Luke stood still and listened. Malc's quiet whirring was mixed with the faint sound of screams coming from the hillside. Luke could tell that they were squeals of delight rather than cries of terror. He was pleased that the kids could enjoy harmless fights in which the worst weapon was merely cold and wet. It made a change for them in this hot-spot of crime.

"Search completed."

"Is there a match?"

"Confirmed."

Eager, Luke said, "Tell me about it, then."

"On Saturday the 16th of July, in the heatwave, a nineteen-year-old woman died from natural causes in Dundee..."

Interrupting him, Luke said, "This one's not entirely natural, is it? She's got a hole in her chest."

"The victim in Dundee was called Emily Wonder."

"What?" Luke exclaimed.

"The victim in Dundee..."

"Yeah. All right. Amazing – having the same name."

Malc paused, churning through statistics. "Given the current population and the number of people called Emily Wonder, the chances of one Emily Wonder being a murder victim are one in five hundred thousand. The probability of a second one being murdered purely by chance is one in two hundred and fifty thousand million."

The numbers were far too big for Luke to take in, but they were telling him that the two deaths were unlikely to be a coincidence. There again, he'd once seen a telescreen programme about a man in Birmingham who'd been struck by lightning three times. The odds against it were astronomical. But it happened anyway. Luke reserved judgement on Malc's mathematical analysis. Apart from the young women's names, there was no obvious link. "Murders in the north are almost unheard of. Anyway, you said that the first Emily Wonder died of natural causes."

"Correct. However, the natural cause was unknown."

"Well, maybe that's another connection. This Emily Wonder didn't die naturally but the cause is unknown," said Luke. "Hand the body over to pathology, Malc. Maybe a full post-mortem will turn something up that we can't see."

"Transmitting."

Feeling miserable, Luke let out a long steamy breath. He hoped that Year Birth in a week's time would bring the madness and extremes to an end.

Chapter Three

Luke felt good. He wasn't getting anywhere with his case but he was in Sheffield with Jade for the Year Birth Concert. He knew that Jade was delighted to see him as well, but she was pretending to be grouchy.

She grumbled, "We haven't seen each other for real in two whole months and, when we do, you bring us to see Emily Wonder. Shall I give you a list of all the things we could do together that'd be better than this? I could've been gigging at a nightclub."

"She's supposed to be high culture, isn't she?" Teasing her, Luke kept quiet about the real reason for coming to a concert by the celebrated opera singer.

"Top warbler, yes. And she's going to warble at us till midnight."

"But you're mad about music."

"Yes, I'm supposed to admire her perfect voice. I do. It's amazing. But I don't want to listen to it for two hours! Amazing and perfect, it is, but it's also unpleasant and unlistenable. Anyway, since when were you into opera? You didn't pick that up in grotty old London."

Luke avoided the question. He shrugged. "I just thought... you know. Year Birth and all that. We ought to do something."

Jade grimaced, clearly not believing him. "Her

screech can shatter glass, you know. She'll probably do the same to my eardrums. And you'd better watch out for Malc. When she turns the volume up for the emotional bits – that's almost all the time – she might blow his casing apart and shake his circuits to bits."

"That is not possible," Malc replied. "There are no frequencies in the human range that can set up harmful resonances…"

Luke interrupted. "Forget it, Malc."

"I do not forget anything. Human memory is poor because a person loses thirty million brain cells over an average lifetime. I am regularly upgraded so my processing capacity increases."

"Show-off," Luke muttered. "Now, shush. It's about to start."

Jade raised her eyebrows. "You sound like Barbara Backley."

Luke was about to ask who Barbara Backley was when the curtain fell back to reveal a singer swamped by a huge green dress.

Jade steeled herself for the ordeal.

Trying to ignore the star's overpowering voice, Luke sat back and thought about two other young women with the same name. He was wondering if his murder victim and the girl from Dundee could be mistaken for the opera singer. Malc had been no use at all. With his sophisticated face-recognition system, he would never confuse them because he could measure numerous points of dissimilarity. But that wasn't the point. It was down to the human eye and Luke wanted to see the singer in the flesh.

He'd checked out Emily's contacts in Woburn and the man who'd discovered her body in the wood. None of them was remotely suspicious and there had not been a breakout from Woburn Prison. Luke hadn't picked up a worthwhile scent. The pathology report hadn't helped with the stabbing weapon. There were no marks on the victim's body, other than the stab wound which had been caused by an unknown round instrument. Unknown. Luke had got fed up of hearing that word. From the wound, the pathologist had concluded only that Emily had been pierced by something clean and about one centimetre in diameter. It had been sharp but it had not scratched her bone.

The pathologist's notes had cleared up one mystery. Emily was an unusual person because she had the condition called *situs inversus totalis*. For every eight thousand normal births, there would be one baby born with this quirk. All of her internal organs were on the wrong side, so her heart lay to the right side of her chest instead of the left. Whoever had killed her was lucky – or knew that she had a wrong-way-round body. The unknown implement had punctured the right ventricle of her heart, leading to rapid death through internal haemorrhage.

Luke had not been assigned officially to the death of EW1, as he and Malc referred to the young woman in Dundee, but he'd made a few informal enquiries. In the sophisticated North, everyone's health was monitored regularly. Samples were taken automatically by smart toilets, sent to diagnostic labs and analysed. An unusual result would be transmitted directly to the person's health centre. According to her medical records, EW1 had died from an unexplained condition while she was perfectly healthy. It didn't seem like natural causes to FI Luke Harding.

On the stage, another EW was warbling and shrieking. Luke was trying not to wince, just like he did when he had to approach a dead body. Around him, most of the audience in the Concert Hall seemed to be awestruck. Jade looked shell-shocked. Luke guessed that she was annoyed. She was annoyed that he'd dragged her along and annoyed with herself for not bringing earplugs.

Luke glanced at her, smiled and squeezed her upper arm. Almost every day he'd spent in the South, he'd seen her image on his telescreen while they chatted, but she was so much more attractive close up. Her nearness made his heart race. If Jade had been in the habit of indulging his tastes, she would have been redheaded for this reunion. But Luke knew that she was too busy in her sound studio and far too independent to pander to him.

Her hair was several shades of blue. It didn't really go with her skin, somewhat lighter than the normal tan, but he loved her for turning her back on convention.

The last two hours of the year seemed everlasting, but eventually Emily Wonder's *tour de force* came to an end with a sustained note that seemed to rattle Luke's brain. She finished exactly on cue as the clock struck midnight. The rapt audience clapped and cheered wildly, Luke and Jade welcomed the birth of a new year with a kiss, and Emily Wonder bowed repeatedly.

When the applause finally faded, Luke whispered in Jade's ear, "I think we should go backstage to meet her."

"What? But..." Jade paused and then nodded knowingly. "This is something to do with your case, isn't it? That's why you brought Malc. You said you've got a dead body, someone called Emily Wonder. You also said you'd come to see me – celebrate Year Birth with me – but you really came to see her! Well, this Emily Wonder's alive and kicking. My poor battered ears prove that."

Luke couldn't deny it. "She was a good excuse, that's all. I wanted to see you, she was appearing here, so... here I am, squeezing as much juice as I can out of the occasion."

"She'll be surrounded by bouncers. You'll never get in. She's famously protective of her privacy."

Luke flashed his identity card. "Remember an FI's power."

Jade was partly right. The corridor was packed with well-wishers, people carrying lavish bouquets, and security staff. Luke, Malc and Jade cut through it all. Inside Emily's dressing room, the overexcited Concert Hall Manager was gushing about the performance. Barbara Backley had both hands to her cheeks as if flushed with emotion. "You are unique. What a voice. Brilliant! Thank you so much." Distracted by Luke and Malc, she turned and said, "Who are you?" There was an accusation in her tone. She appeared irritated that anyone should intrude while she was praising the celebrity singer. It seemed like she wanted Emily to herself. She also seemed to be protecting the star, even from a forensic investigator. Then, seeing Jade Vernon and knowing her as a local musician, she softened her manner. "Ah. Jade. So pleased you were here to see it."

Another woman came up to Emily and handed her a decorative card. Emily read the message and smiled. "Thanks, Freya. Put it with the others."

Realizing that Freya was the singer's assistant, Luke held out his identity card towards the Concert Hall manager and Emily Wonder. "FI Luke Harding."

"What do you want?" Barbara demanded jealously.

Looking at Emily, Luke said, "I need to ask you a couple of things."

Emily nodded as if she'd already figured out his questions. "Yes?"

"I wondered if you've been threatened in the last few

months."

Emily's face changed at once. "But I thought…"

"What?" Luke asked.

"I thought you'd just used your status to get in here to meet me. I thought you were going to ask me about opera, my interpretation and so on. Everyone else does. I didn't know…"

"I'm an investigator," Luke explained. "I investigate."

"What are you investigating? It's twelve-thirty and I've been singing for two hours."

Barbara butted in. "I don't think this is the right time and place…"

At the door, Freya collected another bouquet and thanked someone whom Luke could not see. Freya shut the door and added the flowers to the growing pile.

"I'm sorry," Luke said, "but, if I don't ask now, the opportunity's gone. So, has anyone harassed you or tried to hurt you?"

Emily pulled a face. "I have secret admirers, not enemies." She waved at the mountain of bouquets, "See? People throw flowers at me, nothing else." Then she turned to Barbara and said, "It's all right. You can leave us. I'm sure he won't keep me long."

Barbara frowned at Luke, nodded towards Jade, and then left.

"Why do you want to know?" Emily's voice was quiet and ordinary, unlike her booming vocals when she was on the stage.

"It's just routine security."

"Freya looks after me. She'd know if I got any threatening messages."

From the other side of the room, Emily's minder shook her head.

Emily said, "Check the pile of cards if you like. They're all good will. Most tell me I'm an angel – and quite a few want to pair with me." She smiled sweetly.

"You'll be twenty next year… I mean, later this year. You're coming up to The Time."

"That's right."

Exhausted, the singer was sitting down. She was agreeably plump but a lot smaller than her voice and her stage dress. Looming over her, Luke could tell that she was not tall. He estimated that she was about the same height as Jade. He said, "So, no one's bothered you at all?"

She smiled weakly. "Only an FI after a gruelling performance."

"I'm nearly done," Luke replied. "I guess you move around a lot."

Emily nodded and sipped a fruit drink that Freya handed to her.

"Have you been to Woburn?"

"Woburn?" She looked shocked at the notion. "Isn't it a prison and not much else? I've never been south of Coventry. I don't think people down there would take to me. Or me to them."

"How about Dundee?"

She nodded. "They have a beautiful music hall."

Jade said, "Very fine acoustics."

Emily looked at her for a moment and said, "You're a musician. That's why Barbara knows you."

Jade nodded.

Trying to get back on track, Luke asked, "Were you there – in Dundee – this summer? July?"

Emily wiped away the sweat on her face with a towel and then shrugged. "You'll have to ask Freya. She keeps my diary."

"Never mind," Luke replied. "I can check a database of your appearances. I meant, did you go socially, to see friends or whatever?"

"No." Then, after a pause, she added, "Music's my friend."

"All right. I'll leave you in peace."

Luke was about to leave when Emily said, "Investigator Harding?"

"Yes?"

"You didn't say if you enjoyed my recital."

"Um. It was... amazing voice."

Emily chuckled at his discomfort. "I'm glad you didn't tell me it was fantastic if you didn't like it. I appreciate honesty. What about you, Jade?"

Jade smiled. "Oh, I agree with you. I appreciate honesty as well."

Chapter Four

Wrapped up against the night chill, Luke asked Jade about Barbara Backley. "She seemed a bit... fanatical."

"She's... old-fashioned. A purist," Jade replied, stamping her feet on the pavement outside the concert hall. "She's the type that scowls at anyone who dares to cough during a performance. She didn't have to worry about tonight. The place was deadly quiet – just how she likes it." Jade hesitated before saying, "Anyway, aren't you off-duty now, FI Harding?"

"I guess so." Feeling that he ought to make it up to Jade, he said, "Come on. Let's go out to the hills."

"What? It's one o'clock in the morning! And it's freezing."

"What else are you going to do? Go to sleep? I like the night and I want to see the Peaks covered in snow."

"You won't see much."

"Look." Luke pointed up into the sky. "Plenty of moon. It'll be great. Come on. I could go with you or Malc. You'll be warmer, though."

At once, Malc objected. "I can heat..."

Luke interrupted. "Yeah. But are you warm-blooded?"

"No."

"Will you enjoy snowy hills by moonlight?"

"I do not have the capacity to enjoy anything," Malc answered.

"That's it then. It's got to be Jade."

Malc replied, "I should accompany you."

"Don't you need a recharge?" Luke asked him.

"No."

Luke smiled. "Can't you take a hint?"

"I perform better when given a clear instruction."

"Okay. This has got nothing to do with the case. You go back to the hotel and wait."

Luke's identity card in the freeway reader brought an electric cab to a halt outside the hall. "Where do you suggest?" he asked Jade, as they clambered inside.

"I like Millstone Edge, by Hathersage. There's a viewpoint."

Towards the microphone, Luke said, "The viewpoint on the route to Hathersage."

Immediately, the cab took off at speed. The freeway through Sheffield was busy with noisy revellers celebrating Year Birth. It wasn't like London and the other southern cities. There, late-night antics would be very dangerous and anyone roaming the freeways after dark was not likely to be friendly. Leaving Sheffield behind, a calm settled around them. Suddenly, Luke and Jade seemed to be the only people on the planet.

On Burbage Rocks, high above Sheffield on its south-western side, the new silvery geothermal power station glinted. Three columns of steam rose thickly into the night air from its chimneys. The station pumped cold water five kilometres down into the earth where the planet itself boiled the water. Converted underground into superheated steam, it returned to the surface where it was used to drive a turbine and make the city's electricity. Snow and ice above ground, but red-hot rock below.

Beyond the power station, just before the corridor plunged down to the tiny village of Hathersage, there was a spectacular view over the fells, looking towards Derbyshire. It was cold and crisp and utterly still, like a painting. "Brilliant!" Luke whispered.

"You sound like Barbara Backley talking to Emily Wonder," Jade said with a grin as she grasped his hand.

"I guess I do. It's just that… you know… I don't get this down south." He pulled his hand away from hers and instead wrapped his arm around her shoulders. "And I don't get you. We've got to make the most of our time together."

"You told me you were working on your case in Woburn. You didn't say there was a Dundee connection."

"Another Emily Wonder died there in the summer, but it could've been natural. Maybe it's just coincidence."

"You don't believe that."

Jade had always been able to read his mind. "No."

"Georgia Bowie's in Dundee," said Jade sadly.

Luke looked away from the peaceful sub-zero moorland and gazed at his forbidden girlfriend. He could see that she was bitter about the biologist who would be paired with him. "And there's an artist here in Sheffield. You haven't even told me his name but The Authorities will pair him with you, come The Time."

"Yeah." Having no other words, she hugged Luke instead.

"You never know what the new year might bring."

Jade stared upwards. "Look at the sky."

It was as clear and perfect as the projection that Malc threw onto Luke's bedroom ceiling to help him sleep. He smiled. "I know what you're thinking."

"It's just like the night we left Birmingham. Really starry."

"At school, you said it felt naughty, silly and romantic."

Jade laughed softly. "I don't remember Malc being there, recording what I said."

"I don't need Malc to remember everything that night."

Jade squeezed him. "It's a pity you can't get The Authorities to overhaul the pairing rules now you're an FI."

Luke nodded. "True. But I'm supposed to uphold the law, not change it."

Back in the warm hotel room, Luke looked at Malc and said, "Well? Did you spot anything in Emily Wonder's dressing room?"

"As you requested, I scanned every available surface with visible light. I recorded too many artefacts to read to you. Are you interested in any particular finding?"

Luke smiled. Stating what seemed obvious to him, he said, "Yes. A contact lens. In particular, one that fits the prescription for EW2 in Woburn."

"Not detected."

"That's pretty much what I expected," Luke replied. "If the contact lens shot out of her eye when she was attacked, it could've lodged on the killer's coat. The opera star's coats weren't on view. Anyway, the instruction stands, Malc. Every time I interview someone, scan every accessible surface for the contact lens. If they're wearing a coat, do a fine scan over it."

"Logged."

"I'm not going to ask you for a result every time. Just tell me if you come across it. Right now," he said, looking at the time glowing on the telescreen, "I'm going to bed. If I'm lucky, I'll get to sleep before it's time to wake up."

Instructor Clint Garrett stepped forward with a strange smile frozen on his lips. "This morning," he announced to Edinburgh School's Year 7, "I killed someone." He paused, glaring at every single one of the students, waiting for the shock to sink in. "Murder," he said grimly, as if he were excited, ashamed and proud simultaneously. "I took the knife and held it high over my victim's head." Raising an arm dramatically, he acted out the scene. "She was scared stiff by what was about to happen to her. Totally unable to move. You should have seen the terror on her face. While she was still transfixed, I plunged the knife down deep into her chest and there you are. The deed was done. I threw the knife down and ran away."

Earl Dimmock nudged the girl sitting next to him, nodded towards the window and whispered, "It's snowing again."

"Shush," Tina said, "I'm listening."

"Ooh, sorry, I'm sure."

Tina loved the thick snow, the slides on the hillside, the glassy smoothness of ice, the snowball fights, and breath that came out like steam, but she liked Instructor Garrett's lessons more. Next year, Tina would specialize in criminology. And when she left school, she was determined to be a forensic investigator.

Mr Garrett lowered his arm and broke into a smile. "I'm going to say that a forensic investigator will dash in here in a few minutes with a mobile aid to law and crime and charge me with murder. Why?"

Tina put her hand up. "Because you've left too many clues."

"Like what?"

"Your clothes'll be covered in blood. You've left footprints in it probably. And the knife. It'll be traced to you, especially if you've left fingerprints on it."

Standing in front of the school's bright green wall-hanging, Instructor Garrett smiled. "Exactly. And that's just for starters. A good FI will find a hundred other clues that point straight at me." He hesitated and shook his head. "No. That's not the way to do it. The most important piece of evidence at the scene of any violent crime is the weapon. That's what links the victim to the perpetrator. It always provides clues – fingerprints, traces, manufacturer, supplier – and they all lead to the culprit. So, if I want to be a successful murderer, I don't leave a weapon. And I don't hide it. Hidden weapons are found – sooner or later – by an FI and a mobile. A knife or gun thrown in a lake – not a frozen one," he added with a smirk, "will be found one way or another. Mobiles can perform scans that penetrate water to a depth of a metre or so. Divers can be brought in to search. Sometimes an FI might demand to have a pond or reservoir drained. No. I'm going to tell you, the best way of making sure the weapon's never found is to use one that can be destroyed afterwards without leaving a trace. If I don't want to get caught, I should always destroy the weapon. Without fail. And I don't use a gun because a gun leaves a bullet and that's another link between me and the crime scene."

"What about your clothes, sir? They're covered in blood."

"Burn every last fibre of them. Better still, I wouldn't get blood on them in the first place."

Getting bolder, Tina asked, "So, what *is* the perfect weapon?"

Instructor Garrett laughed. "You had a good idea in your last essay, as I recall. But I'm not here to tell you how to commit the perfect murder, Tina. This is a careers session and I'm giving you a flavour of criminology if you chose to follow it. In one part of the course, I'll show you how an FI deals with a case when there's no evidence of the weapon. It's one of the most difficult jobs an investigator takes on."

Earl's hand went up. "Can an investigator change the law?"

Mr Garrett sighed. "You'd know this if you stopped talking and paid attention, Dimmock. No. Definitely not. It's an FI's job to uphold the law, not to interfere with it. If you want to change the way things are, you need to opt for a different career. Try politics."

Tina knew that Earl was undecided. He'd told her that he was torn between politics and music. His brain urged him to follow the path of politics but his heart was into classical music. Opera was his favourite.

Chapter Five

Emily Wonder leaned on the metal frame beside her bed and got to her feet painfully slowly. A nurse stood by in case she needed help but he didn't offer his arm because, as always, the old lady was determined to be independent.

"That's good. Well done," Alfie said, as if talking to a toddler learning the art of walking. "I've got the sauna all ready. Just how you like it."

Emily shuffled across the room, took a rest, and then tottered a little way down the corridor to the sauna room. The nurse was behind her every step of the way, acting as a safety net in case of a fall.

In the centre of the wood-lined room, there was a fire topped with red-hot coals, like a barbeque inside a cabin. Before Emily made herself comfortable in the seat, Alfie helped her out of her nightclothes, leaving her wrapped in a towelling robe. Then Emily collapsed into the chair with a weary groan.

"You like this, don't you?" Alfie said, holding a vial of Emily's favourite oil.

She nodded gingerly. "Helps with the pain. Gets the joints moving in the morning."

"I'll put it on, then leave you to it." When he placed the small bottle of oil on the coals, the plastic coating melted and there was an angry hiss followed by the smell of sweet herbs. Clouds of white fumes rose up to the ceiling and spread out to fill the room.

From the doorway, the nurse said, "Enjoy."

Emily didn't try to twist her neck towards him because it was too tender, but she found the energy to nod her tired head again. As soon as Alfie shut the door, she closed her eyes, sighed, and then took deep breaths of the powerfully scented air.

The old lady called Emily Wonder was slumped in the only chair in the sauna. If it hadn't been for her utter stillness, she could have been merely napping. She had probably nodded off and died in her sleep because she had made no attempt to get up, pull the emergency cord, fight for her life, or make for the door.

Luke had asked Malc to search databases continuously for deaths or accidents involving women called Emily Wonder. Earlier in the day, Malc had picked up the fatality in York Nursing Home and at once transmitted a request to The Authorities that FI Luke Harding should investigate. He had also made sure that all of the notes on EW1 were handed over to Luke.

"Well," Luke said, "this answers one thing I've been thinking about. The first two Emily Wonders were quite like the opera singer. I reckon someone could have mistaken them for her. But nobody's going to mistake this one for her."

"According to records, she was seventy-eight years old."

"She wasn't attacked, stabbed or shot. But I bet it's not natural causes."

Malc replied, "A doctor certified the death exactly three hours ago. He suspected heart or respiratory failure but has not carried out any tests. He was going to attribute her death to old age until my intervention."

"Mmm. Let's face it, it wouldn't look suspicious to someone who hadn't heard about the other two cases." He wiped his brow as he strolled around the clammy room. "Do you know what I think?"

"No."

"I think she was poisoned."

"Insufficient evidence. Her skin does not show any punctures."

"She could have drunk it or eaten it." Luke stopped by the glowing embers. He looked at the hot coals and then smiled. "Or breathed it in. Someone could have put something on the fire that burnt to a poisonous vapour."

Malc replied, "If combustion of organic material was involved, it will have decomposed."

Luke sighed. "Analyse the air. Perhaps there's a trace of the gas lingering around."

Two minutes later, Malc reported that he had

identified the infrared signature of hydrogen cyanide at the limit of his detection.

"Cyanide poisoning," Luke murmured, stooping to gaze at EW3's inert legs and feet. "I can't smell it, but, yes, she might be pinker than normal. It's hard to tell without knowing her normal colouring. Get pathology to run a toxicity test for cyanide. That would be respiratory failure of a sort – cyanide replacing oxygen in her blood. In a way, she suffocated." He turned to look at Malc. "Death from cyanide gas is very quick, isn't it?"

"Confirmed. Cells are starved of oxygen and death can occur in seconds. Humans are highly unlikely to survive beyond fifteen minutes of exposure."

"EW1 wasn't a cyanide case, was she?"

"No. All toxicity tests were negative. Blood oxygen was normal. All organs ceased to function over several hours."

"Okay. So, how come hydrogen cyanide got into the air? What gives it off if you burn it?"

"Several substances. Some pesticides and nitrogen-containing plastics, particularly acrylic fibres. Wool, silk and nylon. The kernels of peaches, apricots, cherries, almonds and related fruits."

"All right," Luke said. "Bring the pathologists in. I'm going to speak to the staff."

Alfie Dawson opened the large drawer to show Luke

where the sauna oils were kept. "You see," the nurse said, "our residents all like different ones. One or two can't stand perfume, others swear by it. Some want organic herbal treatment, others don't. Anyway, as you can see, they're all labelled for individual residents."

Each compartment of the drawer was clearly marked with a name and filled with small plastic bottles containing mixtures of different waters and oils. Luke's eye went to the section labelled *E Wonder*. "The one you took from here this morning, was there anything different about it?"

"Not that I noticed. Otherwise, I wouldn't have... you know." He looked devastated. He must have realized, from Luke's line of enquiry, that he could have unknowingly supplied the lethal cocktail. "We're all really down because of this. I can't tell you. It's awful."

Luke didn't need to be told. He nodded sympathetically but continued with his questioning. "Who has access to this drawer?"

Alfie shrugged. "It's not locked."

"I'll have to have every vial analysed in a safe lab." He turned briefly towards Malc who was scanning the drawer for fingerprints and other traces. "Get an agent onto it, please."

"Transmitting."

Talking to Alfie again, he said, "Don't use any more bottles and don't let anyone else touch them. I'll also need a list of everyone who works or lives here, and all your visitors."

"Your mobile can access the database of staff and residents. Visitors… That's difficult."

"You don't keep a record?"

"No. We have a lot of residents. That's a lot of friends and partners coming and going."

"Would you – and your colleagues – recognize the regulars, so a newcomer sticks out?"

Alfie shut the drawer and let out a long sigh. "That's asking a lot."

"Where do you get the oils from? Who makes them up?"

"A company called Luxury Health and Beauty."

"Who'd know Emily liked a sauna with oil treatment?"

"Just about everyone. She swore by it. Told everybody who came to see her how good it is."

"How long was she in the sauna?"

"Twenty-five minutes exactly. I set the timer myself. Twenty minutes relaxation therapy, and then the extractor fan comes on to remove steam and vapours. I found her a few minutes after."

"Thanks. That's it for now." Before leaving, Luke hesitated deliberately and said, "Except… It doesn't really matter, but have you been to Woburn recently?"

"Woburn?" The nurse grimaced. "No."

"How about an opera?"

Bemused, Alfie frowned. "What?"

"I can check lists of everyone ordering tickets in this area, but it's a pain. Do you like opera?"

"I'd run a long way to avoid it."

Luke smiled. "I know what you mean. I'm not a fan either. You wouldn't think much of *the* Emily Wonder, then."

Alfie shook his head. "I've heard of her but, no, I doubt if I'd be able to pick her out of a crowd."

As soon as Luke left the building, he said to Malc, "Download attendance lists for all opera performances in every venue in the area for the last year and get that list of staff and patients. Compare the two lists and tell me if anyone's on both."

"Searching."

Swiping his identity card through the freeway reader, Luke said, "Give me the result in the cab. We've got a long journey in front of us. On the way, you'd better book me a room in Dundee. And make sure the hotel's got a supply of pomegranates."

The northward route was unfamiliar to Luke. Thankfully, it was nothing like travelling in the south. From the main corridor that carved through hills, valleys, woods and towns, Luke did not see any derelict buildings, vandalized cabs lying uselessly beside the route, bandits preparing to ambush passengers, or overgrown and disused parks.

Staring out of the window, he said, "You know, I hate cases without a weapon even more than motiveless killings. Both are really tricky. This one's got a motive, even if I don't understand it. Someone's wiping out people called Emily Wonder. But we haven't traced a single weapon. So far, I've got a stabbing with an unknown instrument and a poisoning with an unknown source of cyanide – a hole in the chest and a tiny residue of gas without much of a clue what's behind either. Now, I'm on my way to what's probably an unknown toxin." He shook his head. "It's hard to get off the ground with unknowns."

"Why do you wish to levitate?"

Luke smiled. "I mean, make much progress." Moving on, he added, "You know, if EW1 was murdered as well, and I bet she was, it's time you gave me a roll call on every Emily Wonder in the country. At least the ones that are left. The first three might be just the tip of the iceberg."

Malc hesitated. "I suspect you are referring to a definition of iceberg that is not in my dictionary. Your sentence does not make sense to me."

"It means the three killed so far might be just the start. How many are there?"

"Forty-four."

"Well, we've got plenty of time. Read them all

out. Age, location, career, any known interest in classical music, any health issues, accidents or attacks. I won't be able to memorize it all but I want to hear."

"I have completed the comparison of York Nursing Home and theatre databases."

"And?"

"What do you want me to do with the information?"

"Tell me if anyone connected with the nursing home has gone to the opera."

"Two people."

"Any connection to EW3 or Alfie Dawson?"

"None known."

"Okay. Keep a note of them but, for now, give me what you've got on every Emily Wonder."

Chapter Six

Occasionally, a line of wind turbines that provided power for the automatic cabs chopped the view of hills. High above the corridor, the blades droned in the gale-force wind. Luke watched the wild fells and farms as he listened to Malc's emotionless voice, listing everything he'd discovered from The Authorities' files about each person called Emily Wonder. There were two babies and three pre-school children. Thirteen were at school. The rest were adults and they lived all over the country. Luke expected that he would not have one convenient base for this investigation. He guessed that he'd have to move around a lot, like an opera superstar travelling from one performance to another.

When Malc had finished, Luke said, "I want to talk to three of them. The forensic scientist in Milton Keynes, the Year-10 girl taking criminology at Edinburgh School, and the information technology instructor in Bristol."

"Logged."

"Do The Authorities keep a record of everyone using cabs?" Luke asked. "Can I find out who's been in Woburn, Dundee and York at the time of the deaths?"

"No. That database would be too large to maintain. Also, The Authorities regard it as an infringement of personal freedom to monitor people's movements."

"Pity. Still, it might not have helped because I don't know when the bad vial – if that's what it was – ended up in EW3's drawer. It could have been days, weeks or months ago."

Luke had stripped off his waterproofs and fleece but he was still warm. The heated cab rattled over the Tyne Bridge and began to skirt around the city of Newcastle with its stunning skyline and school famed for sport. Luke added, "I can ask for a particular person's movements to be tracked if it helps a case."

"Confirmed, but I must approve your request. I have criteria requiring firm evidence against an individual before a trace can be applied to their identity card."

"Could I monitor Barbara Backley or Alfie Dawson, the nurse?"

"Not until you have significant evidence against them."

"At least I don't have a problem finding out where Emily Wonder – the singer – goes. I can just check her gig guide. Has she performed in York recently?"

"Yes. Two weeks ago."

"Dundee?"

"She toured between Glasgow, Aberdeen, Edinburgh and Dundee in mid-July last year."

"Mmm. I want The Authorities to send out agents to make sure every Emily Wonder is alive and well. I'd be interested to know if any of them say they've been assaulted."

"Transmitting request."

"I don't suppose The Authorities will give all of them their own minder."

"Do you wish to apply for forty-four bodyguards?"

Luke breathed in deeply. "I might as well, but I think I know the answer."

They passed through a dale draped with snow. In places, deep drifts had collected but The Authorities had kept the corridor clear for cabs. On the slopes of the valley, instructors were holding classes in skiing and a farmer was trudging slowly towards a stranded sheep.

Luke muttered to himself, "What sort of person kills by roll call?" He shrugged. "I'll give him or her the codename Q. That's the letter Q, short for K-E-W, Kills Emily Wonders. Maybe Q's *the* Emily Wonder. Maybe she's so obsessed with celebrity – with being unique – that she's getting rid of everyone else with the same name. But she hardly comes across as completely cracked."

"I did not detect any severe wounds."

Luke laughed. "No. Cracked means mad, bonkers. Maybe she just hides it well. I don't know. It's more likely Q's a stalker or over-the-top fan – someone like Barbara Backley. Didn't she say Emily was unique?"

Malc answered, "She said, 'You are unique. What a

voice. Brilliant! Thank you so much.'"

"Well, killing every other Emily Wonder is one way of keeping her favourite warbler unique. Someone fanatical like her might think she's doing Emily a favour by getting rid of all her namesakes."

"Speculation."

"I don't have anything else right now," Luke admitted. "There might be music reviewers or journalists who've got a strange sort of motive, I suppose. Or the murders might be about one of the other forty-three Emily Wonders and nothing to do with the singer. Maybe one of the others wants to be unique. Maybe one of them wants to be noticed as much as *the* Emily Wonder. Killing makes you famous, in a way. It gets you on the telescreen news more than an opera superstar. If that's right, Emily the celebrity is a target. Q's cunning, though. Not giving me a weapon to work on is very clever. Perhaps it's someone who knows about criminology. That's why I want to interview those three Emily Wonders." He paused before adding, "And I'm hoping EW1 might give me more to go on."

It was a journey marked by grand bridges: Newcastle, Edinburgh and now the major port of Dundee. As dusk closed in, the city loomed on the far bank of the river estuary. Luke's cab sped over the Tay Bridge, three kilometres long, aiming directly at Dundee's heart. Like the bars of a cage, the iron railings either side of him split the darkening scenery.

While the cab turned sharply to the right and ran parallel to Riverside Walkway for a short distance, Malc said, "I have The Authorities' decision on the forty-four bodyguards. It is considered impractical."

"Surprise, surprise."

Malc replied, "Illogical. You expected to be refused."

"Sarcasm, Malc. Look it up. Anyway, here we go."

The electric vehicle slowed to a standstill in the brightly lit cab station and the door slid back automatically. Dundee welcomed them with an icy blast of air.

EW1's body had long since been cremated so Luke and Malc could not inspect it for themselves. Instead, Luke studied the findings and quizzed the pathologist who had conducted the post-mortem. "I'm looking at the possibility that she was poisoned," Luke explained.

The pathologist seemed irritated that his opinion should be questioned by an FI who was thirty years his junior. "Toxicity was negative."

Luke glanced at Malc. "Are there toxins that're lethal at concentrations less than tests can measure?"

"Confirmed."

"For example?"

"Most extremely poisonous substances are made

naturally," the mobile answered. "Ricin is fatal at levels below the limit of detection. One thousandth of a gram is sufficient to kill a human being. It is obtained from the seeds of castor oil bean, *Ricinus communis*. Tetrodotoxin, a poison carried by some species of frogs, newts and marine creatures such as pufferfish, is one of the most toxic substances in the world. It is ten thousand times more lethal to humans than cyanide."

Luke interrupted. "Okay. I get the picture." Turning back to the pathologist, he said, "The question is, if she was poisoned by something you didn't stand a chance of detecting, is there any evidence of how a poison got into her?"

"There were microscopic punctures on her left arm but they were caused by the spines of a cactus. I was thorough. I had them identified. She'd touched a prickly-pear cactus, that's all."

"Any chance there was poison on the cactus spikes?"

The pathologist shrugged. "No way of telling. The inflammation was a normal reaction to cactus spines."

"No other punctures?"

He shook his head.

"How carefully did you look?"

"Very. I always do when the cause of death isn't obvious."

"What about stomach contents? Your report said her last meal was fish."

"Yes. Fish and salad."

Luke asked, "What sort of fish?"

"I don't know, but it wasn't toxic. Salmon's very popular here."

"It might have been pufferfish, with poison below your detection limit."

The pathologist gave a nervous laugh. "Who eats pufferfish?"

Malc replied, "It is a delicacy called fugu in Japan and, on average, it causes a hundred deaths each year."

Dismissing the idea, the pathologist muttered, "This isn't Japan. I've never heard of anyone serving it in Dundee."

Outside the hospital, Luke took a deep breath of the arctic air. "Time to visit an expert," he said. His heart began to thud with misgivings.

Chapter Seven

Georgia Bowie was a good-looking girl, exactly the same age as Luke. She was bright and bubbly. According to The Authorities, she was the perfect partner for him. They were probably right, but the spark wasn't there. Just because they were well matched, it didn't mean that Luke would fall for her. He couldn't fall for her. He was already crazy about Jade Vernon. The mismatch between his profession and Jade's was beside the point. The law forbade their pairing because of it, but his feelings weren't ruled by cold scientific reason. He was certain that he didn't want to spend his life with The Authorities' choice.

Georgia was working at Dundee Animal Sanctuary, just off Riverside Walkway and the elaborate maze of jetties. When Luke had last seen her – at Birmingham School – her auburn hair had been very long. Since then, she'd had it cut smartly to shoulder-length but it didn't come close to Jade's for chaos and colour.

In the muggy and eerie atmosphere of the amphibian house, Luke greeted her awkwardly. "Hi. Happy Year Birth. How's it going?"

Georgia's face lit up when she saw the boy she'd always admired. She reached out and touched his arm affectionately. Then, equally embarrassed, she withdrew it. "Good. And you?"

"Yeah. On a case as always, but I'm fine." He looked around at the shimmering tanks. In the nearest one, harlequin frogs and garish Californian newts were lapping up the artificial sunshine from the lamp overhead. "Nice place to end up."

"No matter what happens out there," she said, nodding towards the exit, "it's always tropical in here. And I get to look after some of the world's weirdest and best-looking creatures."

Luke was about to joke, "Like me," but he decided against it. Instead, he said, "And some dangerous ones?"

"Only if you stick your hand in. And you can't. The displays are sealed. Anyway," she said, "when you said you were coming, you didn't say why."

"Well, it was partly to see you... and partly to ask you something."

She smiled. "Let's go and get a drink." She led the way out of the amphibian house and guided Luke to the canteen. Curious about Luke's work, she asked how he was coping with crime in the South. Then she brought him up to date with her own news. When she'd finished, she paused before saying, "How's..." She stopped, not getting to the end of her question.

Luke guessed that she was going to ask about Jade. He imagined that she changed her mind because she feared hearing that his relationship with Jade had not been dampened by distance.

Georgia shook her head. "Never mind. What was it you wanted to know?"

Luke was relieved. It was easier to talk about murder than it was to raise the topic of their pairing. He told her about EW1 without mentioning her name. He also kept quiet about the other two victims called Emily Wonder.

After listening carefully, Georgia said, "Sounds strange to me. Are you sure she didn't just die in her sleep?"

"Ninety-nine per cent."

"But if she was awake, she'd call for help or shout."

"Normally, yes. But there weren't any reports of noise from her quarters according to the notes I've got, and she didn't make any calls. I still think she was murdered, though."

"People who are being murdered struggle and scream."

"Perhaps she couldn't move or talk."

Georgia frowned, thinking it through.

"That's what I wanted to ask you. I'm wondering about a poison that paralyses before it kills."

Georgia began to nod slowly. "You're right. Tetrodotoxin – or TTX for short."

"That's one on my hit list. Could someone round here get hold of it?"

"You're kidding! You're in Dundee Animal Sanctuary – famous for its amphibians, reptiles and marine life. We've got quite a few species that make TTX. Really, it's not the animals that make it, you know. It's more complicated." She took a sip of her drink before explaining. "You can get it from sea squirts, pufferfish, the blue-ringed octopus, xanthid crabs and that sort of thing, but it's a bacterium called vibrio that lives in their guts that actually makes the stuff. You could get it from the animals or the bugs. It'd be easy for someone who knows what they're doing to grow vibrio in a lab. Easy, but dangerous. You'd end up with a poison factory."

"But people eat pufferfish, don't they?"

With a wicked smile, she said, "Only people who like their main course to come with an element of danger. It's a meal on a tightrope. Fugu poisoning's nasty. You only need a tiny amount of TTX to shut down the nervous system, but it doesn't cross the barrier into the brain. Your daring diner's paralysed and then dies slowly, fully conscious. That fits with what you said about your case."

"Does anyone in the sanctuary take a particular interest in TTX – or the creatures that make it?"

"Not that I know."

Luke hesitated while the attendant came over to take away their empty mugs. Then he asked, "Did any of the poisonous animals disappear in summer? Do you know?

It'd be just before you started work here."

She shrugged. "If it'd happened, the keepers would still be talking about it, I guess. They're not."

Luke asked, "Can I take a look at the animals?"

"Sure," she replied. "You've seen a couple already. You looked in a display with harlequin frogs and Californian newts." She stood up. "Come on. I'll take you to the aquarium. It's in the same building as the amphibians."

The sea-life tanks were bright compared to the passageways between them. The parrotfish, blue-ringed octopus, colourful angelfish and xanthid crabs were housed under ideal conditions. The water, temperature and bubbling air were perfectly controlled, and there was always exactly enough food for them. Even so, each tank was a prison cell for marine life.

"Are they happy?" Luke asked.

"Happy?"

"Mmm. They look good, but wouldn't they prefer the open sea?"

Georgia smiled. "I doubt it. It's a life of luxury in here."

Malc added, "Fish do not have a concept of happiness."

Sadly, Luke said to his mobile, "Like you, I suppose."

"Confirmed."

"Look," Georgia said, pointing. "This puffer's putting

on a display for you." The fish swelled itself up until it looked like a balloon with spikes. "His spines aren't the problem. They're for show. But if they don't put a predator off – if it's still stupid enough to go ahead and lunch on him anyway – it'll die a painful death. The poison's in his skin, liver, guts and reproductive organs."

Keeping his eye on the floating pincushion, Luke replied, "So it's not a brilliant idea to grab him with a bare hand."

"Grabbing a puffer is the last thing you'd do with your life."

Luke examined the aquarium. It was impossible for a visitor to reach the water and the specimens behind the glass. "Sorry, Georgia," he said, "but I need a list of keepers who've got access to these displays."

"That'll be me and a few others. I'll download it to Malc."

"Thanks. Is there anywhere else someone could lay their hands on TTX?" Hesitating, Luke glanced at Malc and said, "I don't mean that literally."

Georgia thought about it. "I suppose so. Some people probably keep pufferfish and the like as pets. A pet supplier's a possibility. Maybe there's a restaurant somewhere that does fugu. Then there's the restaurant supplier. When you think about it, quite a few places."

Luke nodded and sighed. "I'm not exactly flying with this case. Malc, send a message to every restaurant in the area. Ask if fugu's on the menu, or if it was last summer. Then check with the hospital if they've ever had a case of fugu poisoning." He glanced at Georgia and said, "Everyone's got to flash their identity cards to get into the animal sanctuary, haven't they? I did."

"Yes. Why?"

"Does the management keep a log of visitors?"

"No idea," she replied with a shrug.

"Malc. Find out, please. I want to know everyone who came in the day Emily Wonder died."

"Emily Wonder?" Georgia muttered, hearing the name of the victim for the first time. "Not *the* Emily Wonder, obviously."

"No. She's still very much alive and causing earthquakes wherever she sings."

Malc was about to object to Luke's comment when Georgia interrupted. "I think she's great."

The Authorities might calculate that they were right for each other but they could not even see eye-to-eye over music. Luke said, "I'd better get going, Georgia. I've got a few things to follow up. Thanks a lot."

"I don't suppose…"

"What?"

Georgia looked directly into his face. "I don't suppose you've heard from a pairing committee."

She really was attractive and kind. Luke hated the idea of upsetting her. He shook his head. "Right now,

I'm hard to pin down. The Authorities won't know which pairing committee's got to sort me out. But we're four years away from The Time, Georgia."

"Three and a half."

"Plenty of time."

"I suppose so." She stepped forward and, taking him by surprise, kissed him goodbye.

Luke swiped his identity card through the security panel on the block of apartments and went in. Rather than take the elevator, he leapt up the steps two at a time until he reached the third floor. There, he saw a man hanging around outside Emily's apartment. He was short and probably in his thirties but a shaggy beard and peaked cap made him look older. When the man noticed Luke, he dashed into the elevator.

At once, Luke turned round and hurtled back down the stairs to intercept him.

Chapter Eight

On the ground floor, Luke felt foolish. He'd assumed that the man would head for the exit and run from the building, but the elevator had gone up to the eighth floor. Luke sighed and said to Malc, "Give The Authorities a description and get an agent here straightaway. I want a watch on the building till I know who he is."

Luke took the elevator to the eighth storey but, of course, there was no sign of the bearded man in a cap. Instead, Luke went back down to the apartment that, months ago, had belonged to EW1. The new occupants, a couple of elderly actors working at Caird Theatre, stared at Luke's identity card. Startled, the man called Joseph said, "You've left it rather late, if you've come about the girl who was here."

Ignoring the criticism, Luke said, "Did you move in straight after Emily's death?"

"She must have been popular. The corridor was a mass of lilies when she... went. Her brother and a whole host of friends turned up for her cremation. I guess it was... you know... something to do with the way she died. Horrible."

Often, after a death, there would be a memorial service to celebrate a person's work and life, but EW1 hadn't lived long enough for that. At least her passing had been marked by those who knew her. Luke wished he'd been able to join them. Right now, he just wanted an answer to his question. "You moved in afterwards. When, exactly?"

"We've changed the place around a bit, but we didn't have to. She kept it really nice, didn't she, Cherelle?"

Clearly, the actor did not feel bound by a forensic investigator's questions. He used them as an excuse to talk about anything that struck him as important or interesting. His partner seemed content to nod, agreeing with everything he said.

"How long after she died did you move in?"

"No one wanted it at first. I guess it was... you know... because of someone dying here, but a place doesn't define a person, does it, Cherelle? A person defines a place, particularly their own living space. That's what we believe. There's nothing left of her – or her fate. Just because she met a terrible end here, it doesn't mean... you know. We're not worried."

In frustration, Luke glanced around the living quarters. It was an unfussy apartment. Light and plain in colour, giving it a clean and airy atmosphere. The sofa was new, not the one that cushioned Emily as she drifted helplessly to death. Through the window blinds, he could see a small jam-making factory to the right and a fabric design department to the left. Beyond, an autoship was wheeling slowly towards one of the landing stages at the edge of the Tay. "The place wasn't stripped before you moved in?"

Possessions weren't held in high regard because they could be easily replaced. At the end of a life, they weren't inherited by the dead person's family. They were usually recycled into the community by The Authorities.

"As I said," Joseph began again, "we've rearranged a few things but it's still much as it was. We haven't..."

Interrupting the relentless flow, Luke asked, "Was anything removed?"

"People don't always have the same tastes, do they? A wall-hanging, a piece of sculpture, a certain style of chair. They might look gorgeous through one person's eyes, but through another..."

"So, what did you get rid of?"

"We're not great animal-lovers, are we, Cherelle? The animal embroidery went and she had quite an aquarium..."

"An aquarium? Do you happen to know what sort of fish she kept?"

"We're actors. We know every play you're likely to..."

"But you don't know fish?" said Luke, trying for a shortcut to the answer.

"I'm sure fish have their merits – I suppose some

people would think they're beautiful. Serene, perhaps. We're more likely to recognize them when they're served on a plate. You see, fish can't throw much light on the human condition..."

Now, Luke was getting annoyed with Joseph's habit of turning every reply into an earnest and rambling speech. "What did you do with the aquarium?"

"As I said, people don't always take pleasure in the same things. We're sure there are lots of people out there who'd appreciate a fish tank, so we called in Dundee Pet Supplies and they took it away. We hope that the fish found a good..."

Luke decided to dive in and change the subject. "Have you seen a short man with a beard and cap in the building?"

"I suppose everyone looks short to you..."

"But have you seen someone like that?"

"I don't think there's any harm in him. He's never bothered us anyway. He lives upstairs somewhere. I don't know who he is, but he skulks about the place like a lost and tormented soul. It's like he's stalking someone after they're dead. He's more tragic than threatening in our view. I get the impression he's still obsessed with Emily Wonder. Not *the* Emily Wonder, you understand. The one that..."

"Thanks," Luke said, trying to bring the tiresome conversation to an end. "That's all. But, just one last thing. When did you say you moved in here?"

At last Cherelle said something. "It was two weeks after Emily's death, Investigator Harding. Poor girl."

Luke nodded and smiled.

Luke did not need Malc to project the image of a starry night onto his bedroom ceiling. He could look out of the window into the sub-zero night and see a vast expanse of clear sky. To reach his eyes this night, light from the stars had set out billions of years ago. It always struck him as bizarre that he was seeing how the stars looked a very long time ago. "EW2 in Woburn was trained to be a food technologist – maybe a chef – so search all information in case you can find out if she ever prepared fugu, though I don't know what that's got to do with EW1. Or EW3."

"Searching."

"What was EW1's job?"

"Textile designer."

Luke nodded. Dundee had a strong history in the production of fancy fabrics. "And EW3?"

"What is your query?" Malc asked.

"She was retired – obviously – but what did she work in?"

"She was a gardener."

"Did she specialise in cacti, by any chance?"

"Confirmed."

Puzzled, Luke thought about it. "A retired cactus grower in York, a food technologist in Woburn, and a fabric designer in Dundee. Only obvious link: their name. But EW1 could have been poisoned by a meal of fish, or something sprinkled on a cactus."

Malc reported, "It is highly unlikely that Emily Wonder in Woburn ever made fugu. She helped to prepare meals in Woburn and Milton Keynes. In that area, restaurants are not sophisticated enough to offer fugu."

"How about Dundee? That's a different kettle of fish altogether."

"Kettles and fish are relevant to your current line of enquiry, but my programming fails to find a rational meaning."

Luke turned away from the stars and smiled at his mobile. "Dundee restaurants are in a different league — much more stylish. Did you find one serving puffer?"

"No. In addition, the hospital has never recorded a case of fugu poisoning."

"Was there a list of visitors to the animal sanctuary? Did you download it?"

Malc answered, "Confirmed. I have stored it."

"Did EW1 go the day she died?"

"Confirmed. She arrived at eleven-nineteen and left at one-fourteen."

"Two hours," Luke muttered to himself.

Correcting him, Malc said, "One hour and fifty-five minutes."

"Whatever. I wonder if she ate there."

"She presented her identity card for lunch in the canteen."

Luke sat up straight. "Interesting. Keep a list of everybody who was in the sanctuary at the same time. Have their names cropped up in any of the three EW cases so far?"

"No."

Luke sighed. "Was the animal sanctuary one of the canteens you checked for fugu?"

"Yes."

That meant it had not served EW1 with pufferfish. He gazed out of the window for a minute and then asked for a link to Jade. Almost at once, Malc threw her image onto the bedroom wall.

"Hiya," she said. "How's tricks?"

"Could be worse."

"Where are you? I can't keep up."

"Dundee."

She hesitated for a moment. "Dundee. Have you seen Georgia?"

Luke could not tell her a lie. "Yes," he replied. "All in the line of duty. She helped me with that case up here."

"Is she as gorgeous as ever?"

Luke smiled wryly. "If you like that sort of thing, yes."

"And as keen on pairing with you as ever?"

"I put her off for a bit." Changing the subject, he said, "Have your ears recovered from the Year Birth concert?"

"Barely. When I shut my eyes, I can still hear her screeching."

Luke laughed briefly. "Can you keep a secret?"

"You know I can."

"Why does anyone kill people with the same name, Jade?"

She shrugged. "I don't know. To terrify the last one standing, maybe."

"Mmm. How would you feel if someone started bumping off other Jade Vernons?"

"How could there be anyone else like me?" she replied with a grin. "I'm a one-off."

"Seriously."

"Scared stiff."

Luke nodded. "Emily with the amazing throat didn't seem scared stiff to me."

"So, she hasn't heard about the other Emily Wonders. You didn't let on."

"That means whoever's doing this can't be trying very hard to terrify Emily Wonders. Q – the killer – isn't making a song and a dance about it."

Malc interrupted. "To avoid detection, Q is unlikely to indulge in such behaviour."

Jade clapped her hands. "Absolutely right, Malc.

How could you make such a silly suggestion, Luke?"

"Shush. Malc's bad enough without you encouraging him. Anyway, I think you're wrong about the motive."

"Okay. Maybe Q thinks he can get at one Emily Wonder by hurting her namesakes. You know. Like a voodoo doll. You stick a needle in the doll and the real person feels the pain."

"Mmm. Scientific nonsense," Luke replied, "but an interesting idea."

"If it was me," Jade said, "I'd do us all a favour and throttle just the one Emily Wonder. Pure and simple."

Malc reported, "An agent has identified the bearded man as he returned to his quarters this evening."

"I've got to go, Jade. You take care."

"You too."

When her image faded, Luke turned to Malc. "What's his name, then?"

"Cornelius Prichard."

"Did he visit Dundee Animal Sanctuary on the day EW1 died?"

"Confirmed."

Luke smiled with satisfaction. "Now I'm humming."

"I do not detect any sound."

Ignoring his mobile, Luke said, "Come on. Interview time."

Chapter Nine

It was after midnight. Luke had got Cornelius Prichard out of bed to talk to him. Without his cap, the man looked entirely different. His hair, like his beard, was jet black and rugged. His cheeks glowed pink as if he were constantly drunk or embarrassed. Even though he must have been drowsy, his bright eyes darted warily between Luke and Malc.

"I'm investigating a disturbance on the third floor," Luke said to him. "Do you ever go down there?"

"I... er... Yes, but I haven't done anything wrong," he replied. "Not a thing."

"Where do you go? And why?"

"It's... er... awkward."

Luke could see that he had suddenly begun to sweat. "I need an answer."

Prichard's eyes flitted towards Malc. He must have known that the mobile was recording the interview. "I heard about Emily Wonder and... you know."

"What?"

"I was fascinated. That's why I moved into this block. To be closer to her." His cheeks had become bright red now.

"But you must know she's died."

Cornelius nodded. "I mean, closer to where she was. You see, I'd broken my arm. I was in plaster when I first met her."

Cutting in, Luke asked, "Where was that?"

"The animal sanctuary. In the canteen. She died a few hours later, according to the news." He shook his shaggy head. "Awful. Dreadful."

"If that was the first time you met her, how come you knew who she was?"

"She left her identity card on the table next to mine. You don't forget a name like Emily Wonder. No way. I dashed after her and gave it back."

"Was that the last time you saw her?"

Cornelius stared at Luke nervously. "Yes. I didn't follow her. Nothing like that. But, when I heard she'd died, she sort of... haunted me. I might have been the last one to see her alive. And she was so young. Such a waste. I can't get her out of my mind."

"Did you see what she was eating in the animal sanctuary?"

Cornelius looked baffled. "Er... no."

"What did she say to you?"

"She scratched her arm on a cactus by the door and I told her she'd be all right." He sighed heavily, looking even more guilty. "Then she asked me what I wanted. When I gave her her identity card, she said, 'Silly me. Thank you.' Such a lovely young voice. It's... more than a shame."

"And that's why you moved in here? To be close to the

memory of someone you barely knew?"

"You make it sound… crazy. But it didn't feel like that to me. You see, I feel like I really connected with her. I'm not a stalker or anything. No. I can't stalk someone who's not around any more. But I am a bit obsessed, I suppose. She… affected me."

Luke nodded. He didn't really understand Cornelius Pritchard's obsession, but it wasn't against the law to be weird. His story seemed to check out with everything that Luke knew about EW1's final day. "It wasn't a nice way to die, was it?"

"I don't know how she died. Only what they said on the local news. It sounded long and painful, I'm afraid. What killed her?"

Luke's only answer was a shrug. "What's your job?"

"I'm a builder."

"Did you go into her apartment?"

Cornelius shook his head.

"Or get a look inside?"

"Once. When I left some lilies."

"Did you see a fish tank?" Luke asked.

"Emily kept fish?" He was grateful for any extra information about her because, after her death, he'd claimed her as a friend. "No. I didn't know that. I didn't see it."

"Have you heard of *situs inversus totalis*?"

Cornelius frowned and shook his head. "Was she ill?"

"No. Forget it." Luke put on a shiver. "I'm going to have to go out again in a minute. It's cold, isn't it? I bet you need good winter coats up here."

Cornelius gazed at him, mouth open.

"It'd be helpful if I could take a quick look at them."

"In there." He pointed to a cupboard near the front door.

Luke opened it so that Malc could scan inside for a contact lens, then he prepared to leave. "Thanks. That's it for now. But, off the record, something's been troubling me."

"Oh?"

"Haven't I seen you before?"

"I don't know. Have you?"

"I've just come from York. Have you been there?"

"A long time ago," Cornelius answered.

"How about further south? Maybe that was it. Just before Year Birth. Weren't you in Woburn?"

"I don't think so."

"Maybe you were building down there?" Luke nodded in Malc's direction and said, "I can check."

"I've never been to Woburn. No chance."

After a pomegranate breakfast, Luke went back to the restaurant in the animal sanctuary. Finding the chief attendant, he asked, "Were you working here last summer?"

The woman nodded. "Yes, sir."

"Do you happen to remember serving someone called Emily Wonder?"

"No, but…"

"What?"

"One of my colleagues did. Roxy. He kept talking about her. Still does, actually. We don't normally remember customers but, well, she died and her name… you know. I guess it fixes it up here." She tapped the side of her head.

"Can I speak to him?"

She pointed towards the young man wiping down tables. "That's him."

Roxy still recalled asking the young woman if she was *the* Emily Wonder and then serving her meal. "Salmon salad, I think it was, but…" He shrugged. "I can't be sure."

"Did anything unusual happen to that meal?"

Roxy frowned. "Unusual? What do you mean?"

"You took it from the kitchen, straight to her table?"

"Yes."

"So, no one could've interfered with it."

Roxy shook his head. "Not without the chef, me or her knowing about it."

"Did she leave her table at any point?"

Roxy stared at the ceiling, thinking. "Yes. Before the meal was ready, I think. I guess she went to the washroom."

"Do you remember anything odd happening? Anything at all."

Roxy shrugged. "Not really."

Luke pounced. "That means something happened but you don't think it matters."

"Well…"

"Tell me."

"I'm sure it's… nothing. I didn't mention it to the investigator – he didn't seem very interested anyway – but it made me think afterwards. When I served her meal, after she'd come back to the table, she pointed to a bottle of water and said thanks."

"Yes?"

"Well, I didn't put it there. It didn't strike me as important. It was thirsty weather back then. Very thirsty. I guessed she'd asked another attendant for it but thanked me instead. It's common enough. It's just that… because she died… it's stuck in my mind."

Luke nodded. "Thanks. That's helpful."

On his way out, Luke paused by the shelf of cacti and shook his head. No one would lace the spines with poison on the off chance that the intended victim would stumble into them. But that bottle of water intrigued him. It would have been easy for someone to lace it with a tiny amount of TTX and then place it on her table when she slipped out to the washroom.

Chapter Ten

Before leaving for Edinburgh on Saturday, Luke visited Dundee Pet Supplies but none of the staff could recall receiving an aquarium the previous summer following its owner's death. No wiser about the fish that EW1 kept, Luke took a cab and headed south. He was keen to talk to the Emily Wonder who was a Year-10 student taking criminology at Edinburgh School.

The building was a granite monster that looked as if it had stood on the site for ever. The interior was a blend of the ancient and the luxurious. The ornate ceiling was a long way above Luke's head. It had been painted green to match the curtains. In the reception, it was an Instructor Clint Garrett who greeted him with a powerful outstretched hand. "So, you're the famous Luke Harding, then." His voice echoed around the large room.

"Famous?"

"Famously young for an FI. Word about you reached us from Birmingham. I cancelled a hill-walking weekend to meet you. Of course," he said with a sly smile, "you might not hold the record of the youngest FI for long. I can tell you, we have a batch of bright students ourselves."

To Luke, the instructor seemed more than usually competitive. "Does that include Emily Wonder?"

"Perhaps, but… Never mind. You'll see for yourself. I guess you want to get on and meet her."

"Please."

Leading Luke down a hushed passageway, Instructor Garrett said, "Does she have anything to worry about?"

"How do you mean?"

"Am I correct in thinking it's about the death of three people with her name?"

Luke grimaced. "Not many people know about that."

"I'm in criminology," he explained. "I've got a computer program that searches all local news broadcasts for crime and it's come across the name of Emily Wonder three times."

"There's no sure evidence to say they're crimes."

Clint Garrett laughed. "Oh yes there is. One: it's too much of a coincidence to be natural. Two: an FI turns up at my school wanting to speak to our own Emily Wonder."

"Have you told her about your research?"

"Yes. I couldn't live with myself if something happened to her and I hadn't warned her." He turned into a small meeting room and said, "Ah, here she is. Emily, this is FI Luke Harding."

"Thanks," Luke said to him, trying not to react outwardly to the student's strange appearance. "You can leave us." He waited until Mr Garrett had closed the door before asking with a smile, "Is he a good instructor?"

Her answer lacked enthusiasm. "Nowhere near as good as he likes to think."

"There's a few like that."

"He rates himself as my friend but…" She didn't have to say any more. The slight sneer on her face was enough.

She was the strangest looking girl Luke had seen. She was incredibly thin. Her body and face seemed to consist only of sharp angles. Her skin was like a brown plastic bag stretched over bone and muscle. She was also far too tall – even taller than Luke – and her huge chin jutted out unnaturally. At a glance, she looked masculine. But her eyes reminded Luke of his own. She was examining him carefully like a mobile aid to law and crime scanned a suspect. Probably eager to find out the purpose of his visit, she was looking for clues in his manner.

"I bet he tells you how murderers try to fool investigators. They all do."

"He goes on about the motiveless and weaponless killing of a stranger," she replied. "Then there's nothing to link the culprit to the victim – or the crime scene."

Luke asked, "How do you commit a weaponless murder?"

"I don't," she said in a deadly serious voice.

"How *would* you?"

Emily fidgeted in her seat. "Are you testing me?"

Luke shook his head. "I'm just curious about how they train you here."

Emily shrugged. "A poison that works at very low levels, maybe. Something biological like a virus. Chemically, potassium chloride's a classic. Stops the heart but doesn't leave a trace."

"Except a puncture wound."

"An injection inside the mouth is very hard to spot."

Luke grinned. "The would-be victim might notice someone trying to shove a needle down her mouth."

"Stun with a stinger first, then."

"Okay. Forget chemical and biological stuff. What about a physical weapon that kills but doesn't leave a crumb for an FI? The stream of electrified air from a stinger hits like lightning, leaving a burn mark."

Emily thought about it for a few seconds. "Is there one?"

"Probably not," Luke replied. He took a deep breath. "Anyway, to business. I guess you know what this is about. Mr Garrett's told you three people called Emily Wonder have died in suspicious circumstances in the last six months."

She nodded. Waiting for Luke to say more, she grasped each finger of her left hand in turn with the thumb and forefinger of her right hand. It was probably a habit and it emphasized the length and odd shape of her bony hands.

Luke knew that if Jade were with him, she'd argue that Emily was bound to be edgy, maybe even terrified. But Luke had to be more suspicious than that. She might be tense because she was Q. She certainly knew more than most about how to make a forensic investigator struggle. "I'm afraid The Authorities don't have the resources to give you and every other Emily Wonder a bodyguard. I'm sorry. You need to be careful."

"How did they die?"

"I can't say," Luke replied.

"How can I watch out if I don't know what to watch out for?"

"Whoever did it didn't leave much by way of clues."

Emily nodded. "They were weaponless and motiveless. That's why you asked me."

"I'm telling you about it because the only motive seems to be the name of Emily Wonder."

She took a deep breath. "So you're looking at Emily Wonders not just as potential victims but possible perpetrators."

Clearly, she was sharp as well as serious. "Yes," he admitted.

Emily toyed with her long misshapen fingers again. "And I'm more likely to be a suspect than a victim because I know criminology."

"Have you been absent from school recently? I can get Malc to log on to school records, but it's easier if you just tell me."

Apparently unwilling to answer, Emily paused uncomfortably. Finally, she said, "As you can tell, just by looking at me, I'm ill. I've had to have quite a lot of time off."

Luke was too tall and wiry to be considered a classic male. But no one would ever think of him as ugly. Emily was sadly unattractive, with her bulky lower jaw, extreme height, and deformed bones. Sympathy in his voice, he asked, "What's the problem?"

"Get your mobile to scan my face. He'll tell you."

Malc recognized the shape at once. "The bone structure is highly characteristic of lipodystrophy. It is a rare genetic disorder in which a patient is born without any body fat. The condition causes hormone imbalance, resulting in excessive growth and distortion of facial bones." Unlike Luke, Malc could not mix compassion with facts.

"He's right," Emily added. "Fat's a vital body tissue, keeping us healthy, but I don't have any."

She deserved pity, Luke thought, but he doubted that she would want him to make a show of it. "I'm sorry," he said. Then he tried to carry on normally. "What do you do with all this time off?"

"Lie in bed, sleep and groan, mostly," she replied, as if annoyed that Luke hadn't taken in the severity of her condition.

"You don't travel?"

"Huh. If only I could," she exclaimed.

Luke had no way of checking because The Authorities didn't keep a file of cab use, but there was no doubting that she was seriously ill. He asked, "What's it like to be an Emily Wonder?"

"Tedious. Everyone expects me to be a good singer and I have to put them right all the time." She shrugged helplessly. "Talent's got nothing to do with your name."

Luke stood up. "I'll tell you what. Next time I see the singer, I'll ask if she's any good at criminology because she's got the same name as Emily Wonder at Edinburgh School."

At last, Emily heard something worthy of a smile. "Good idea. I'd like that."

Before leaving Edinburgh, Luke asked to see Clint Garrett again in private. Luke said, "I got the impression you thought Emily was really bright but wouldn't make a young FI. Why's that?"

The instructor took a deep breath. "You saw her. You should be able to guess."

In a soft voice, Luke said, "She's not expected to live long enough to take the final qualification exams?"

Plainly upset, Mr Garrett nodded. "It's cruel. A tragedy. She's a good girl. Very clever, very brave. But her prospects aren't good, according to the medics."

Saddened, Luke muttered, "Pity."

Chapter Eleven

In the cab, Malc recited the post-mortem findings on all three victims. It didn't take long because there wasn't much to report. EW1, textile designer in Dundee, died in July, unknown natural causes. EW2, food technologist in Woburn, killed in December, stabbed by an unknown implement that did not leave any residue. EW3, retired gardener in York Nursing Home, died in January, poisoned by hydrogen cyanide generated by burning an unknown substance.

A chemical laboratory had analysed every vial of oil in York Nursing Home and they were all perfectly innocent, all perfectly safe. The traces on the drawer containing the vials led only to the nurses. If a visitor had placed the fatal bottle of oil in EW3's section of the drawer, the intruder must have used gloves and left only one contaminated vial. Enquiries at the company that made the sauna oils, Luxury Health and Beauty, had drawn a blank. It was exactly what Luke expected and dreaded. He had grown used to blanks and unknowns in this case.

Malc had also received the agents' statements on all living people called Emily Wonder. He had plenty of time to read out the roll call to Luke because, on its way to Milton Keynes, the cab made a large detour around a blocked corridor at Northampton.

There was only one report that grabbed Luke's attention. The youngest of the three Emily Wonders in London had gone missing. It was nothing new for people in London to vanish for a while – and sometimes permanently – but this eleven-year-old girl was called Emily Wonder. That made her special, very different from all of London's other missing people. Luke decided that he would investigate her disappearance as soon as he could.

The cab slowed as it entered the dangerous network of crisscrossing freeways in Milton Keynes. On the northern side of the town, there was a large monument to the endangered cat family. The tall column was made up of interwoven concrete cats. Once, it had been a striking feature of the community, but vandals and weather had eroded it. Now, it was hard to distinguish a leg from a tail, and a few heads had been removed altogether. Beyond the concrete cats, the neglected theatre and ski centre were covered in dirty snow. The food warehouse had a huge hole in one side where bandits had attached sticks of dynamite and blown away the bricks to get access to the store.

Luke's identity card was always in credit because he worked hard. He could get everything he wanted. But, in the south, it was often more difficult to find a job than to join a group of bandits. In many towns, identity cards had ceased to be the local currency. Force, cunning and a desperate form of courage had taken their place. Milton Keynes was a far cry from Sheffield, Dundee and Edinburgh.

Luke paid a visit to the forensic scientist who lived in the one safe part of town and learned straightaway that she hated her name.

"I'm sick of being Emily Wonder," the thirty-year-old said angrily, "and I'll never sing a note. I could, but I won't. That's my protest. It's a nightmare. Every time I use my identity card, I get it. 'Emily Wonder? Really? You're amazing,' or, 'Emily Wonder. I've heard of you. Not exactly my thing but... Hold on. I'll just go and get my mate. She's a huge fan of yours,' or, 'Emily Wonder? You don't look much like her. Still, give us a tune.' I can't stand it."

She'd been to most of the northern cities – attending courses on forensic science and taking a break from Milton Keynes – and she'd also been called to Woburn recently to gather evidence about a disturbance in the prison. She'd heard of tetrodotoxin and knew its sources, but she'd never worked on a case where it was a suspected poison. Trained in chemistry, she knew how to generate cyanide gas as well.

Plainly, she had the knowledge to murder the first three Emily Wonders. Because she'd travelled, she might also have had the opportunity. And because she detested having the same name, she had a motive.

Even so, two things did not add up in Luke's mind. He was not persuaded that the forensic scientist was a serious suspect. Afterwards, talking to Malc, he explained, "First, she didn't try to hide the fact that she's got the know-how and maybe had the chance to kill. She didn't try to cover up being annoyed. Second, she's got it in for the opera star, not the others. If she got to breaking point, she'd go for Emily the singer."

Luke could not face another long journey to another seedy city. He conducted his next interview by telescreen in his hotel room. The information technology instructor in Bristol looked very similar to the superstar singer, with five years added on. Unlike the forensic scientist, she was tense because she already knew about the three deaths. She said she'd come across them while she was searching on-line databases to discover her family tree.

Luke was puzzled. "Family tree?" he queried.

"I know it's unusual," she replied, "but some of us are still curious about where we came from. You leave your parents behind when you go to school. It's like... I don't know... shutting a door on your history. I got a fix on my grandparents and their parents. Now, I'm going another generation back. It's not easy."

Luke was surprised. He couldn't remember the last time he'd heard anyone use the word 'grandparent'. It wasn't something that people talked about. It wasn't considered important because it was all behind them.

Luke knew he was the result of the pairing of the astronomer, Elisa Harding, and his doctor father, Peter Sachs, but he had no idea where his parents were now. He'd never asked Malc to consult the right records. He hoped that they were alive and well. When they'd handed him over to the school at the age of five, he had been disconnected from them, like every other new student leaving their mother and father. If Luke's little sister hadn't died at such a young age, he would have kept in touch with her as she went through the same school. He would have liked that. And it was normal for some brothers and sisters to stay in contact. For most, that was the extent of it. The Authorities took the place of a family. Yet Luke had a secret wish to meet his mother and father again. One day, he imaged saying, "Here I am. It's Luke. This is how I turned out." He liked to think that they'd be proud of their son. He liked to think that they'd enjoy meeting Jade as well. It was just a dream, though.

The Emily Wonder in Bristol was intent on researching her own dream, her own roots. Plainly, she didn't think of the activity as a waste of time and effort, even though most people would find it mystifying and pointless.

"It's interesting," Emily insisted. "It's not too difficult to trace back from a mother to grandmother – because you've got the family name and birthplace to work on – but grandfathers and further back are really tricky. There just isn't the software and archives to do it. If I'd got an uncommon family name, it'd be less of a problem."

Luke decided to drag her back to his case. "I'm into fish more than families."

"Oh?"

He watched her image carefully as he deliberately confused the vibrio bacterium with a fish. "Yes. Vibrio's a favourite."

Emily stared blankly back at him from the screen projected onto the wall. She did not react to the mention of the poisonous bacterium that produced TTX and she did not correct his mistake.

Behind Luke, Malc began to point out his error. "Vibrio is not a…"

Luke put up his hand. "Never mind. Have you heard of *situs inversus totalis*?"

"Is it a fish?"

Luke smiled and shook his head. "Someone said you'd been up to York recently."

"York?" Emily frowned. "I'm sure it's very nice, but I haven't been there. I don't know where you heard that."

"Oh. How about Woburn?"

"Yes. I took a small group of our most troublesome students there. A prison visit. It's supposed to put them off crime but... I don't know. They never think they're going to get caught."

Luke nodded. "Why did you choose Bristol anyway? It's..."

"Rough?" she suggested.

"Yeah."

"I'm here *because* it's rough. It's places like this – and these sorts of kids – that need good instructors. I think I can make a difference. If every decent instructor went to Birmingham or further north, what'd happen to children down here?"

"Point taken," Luke replied. He believed that she was harmless. More than that, she seemed to be too caring to be a murderer. He didn't have to warn her to be careful because she was already aware of the risk of being an Emily Wonder. Instead, he said, "I'd better let you carry on climbing your family tree. Thanks."

Luke watched the image fade and let out a long sigh. "Tomorrow morning," he announced, "I'll go back to Sheffield."

Malc asked, "For what purpose?"

"I need to have a chat with Barbara Backley. And it's in the middle of the three murder scenes so it's as good a place as any to base myself." He decided not to add that he was missing Jade again. "After that, back to London.

It's worth looking into the Emily Wonder who's disappeared."

It was Sunday and Luke could not work on his bizarre case endlessly. He needed a break so, when Jade suggested that they take advantage of the diabolical weather and go ice-skating, Luke agreed at once.

The boating lake at Graves Park was completely solid. Swans were looking at the transformed water in bewilderment. The rowing boats had been dragged out of the lake and lay on the bank like beached whales. Hand in hand, Luke and Jade glided across the frozen surface as effortlessly as Malc hovered at Luke's shoulder. The place wasn't crowded but several groups of people were taking the opportunity to skate. A mother and father, with a baby in a pushchair, were watching their older son testing his sense of balance on the ice. Not yet school age, he giggled aloud every time he fell down. Two girls were shouting to each other and screaming whenever a boy on the path threw a snowball at either of them. At the other end of the lake, four boys had made a treacherously slippery slide from one bank to another. They were running over the snow-covered grass, jumping onto the slide and skidding all the way across to the opposite edge.

Leaving Jade for a moment, Luke skated towards the end where the boats had been arranged side by side.

The small boy, still unsure on his legs, waved his arms and began to totter again. Out of control, he veered unexpectedly and then fell right in front of Luke.

To avoid hurting the toddler, Luke leapt into the air and flew over him. Luke dropped back down onto the ice, lost his balance and crashed into the bank, shin first. He let out a cry of pain and sprawled onto the cushion of snow at the edge of the lake, his head narrowly missing one of the rowing boats.

Rolling over with a groan, his face ended up centimetres away from a sizeable and sturdy icicle dangling from the prow of the boat. Immediately, he forgot about his bruises.

Chapter Twelve

Kneeling beside Luke, Jade asked anxiously, "Are you all right?"

Luke nodded. "Fine." Sitting up, he grabbed the icicle in his gloved fist and wrenched it from its moorings on the lip of the boat. "What's that?"

"Nice, isn't it?" Jade replied. "I think icicle is the technical expression for it. Are you sure you're okay?"

"It's a hefty spike."

"Are you concussed or something?"

Luke weighed it in his hands and then examined it. Sharp at the lower end, strong and broad at the top. "It could be a dagger."

"A dagger? No. Not unless you've got a very warped mind."

"Like the sort of mind that goes around killing people called Emily Wonder?"

"All right. To someone like that, it's a dagger."

"Malc," Luke said. "I want some fresh pork for an urgent forensic test."

"Pork?" Jade cried. "Now I know you've got concussion."

Luke collected an icicle from a bare branch of the tree outside his hotel and dashed inside with it before it melted. He had already laid the leg of pork on the table. "When they test the damage bullets and other weapons do to people, they use dead bodies. If they haven't got any, they experiment on pigs," he said. "A pig's not that different in structure to a human."

"This is a valid experiment," Malc confirmed.

Luke lifted up the icicle, sharp end towards the meat, and drove it down as if he were stabbing the animal. The glassy point penetrated the tough skin and slid easily into the flesh. The improvised weapon hit the leg bone, glanced off it, and came to a halt only when it pierced the skin on the underneath and struck the tabletop.

Luke let go of the icicle and said in triumph, "There you are. A very clever dagger. Strong enough to do the job but, once it's in a nice warm body, it just melts away. No fingerprints, no trace at all. It'd mix with the blood and body fluids. People are seventy-five percent water anyway, so a bit more isn't going to be noticed, not even by you."

Malc agreed. "Correct."

Luke eased the transparent blade out of the joint of meat. "Scan the wound and compare with EW2's injury."

Malc positioned himself over the leg of pork, measured the hole, and examined the damage done to the skin, the underlying layers of tissue and muscle. "The formation of the lesion is the same in both cases," he stated.

At last. Luke believed he had eliminated one unknown. Smiling broadly as he dropped the icicle into the sink, he said, "I think we know what killed EW2 in the wood."

"Not proven," Malc replied, "but highly likely."

Returning to the leg of pork, Luke added, "I think we know what's for dinner tonight as well."

Having got used to the slums of the South, Luke regarded Jade's quarters as fantastic. The whole building seemed spotless, warm and elegant. Her apartment was perched, ten floors up, on a hill overlooking Sheffield. Beyond it lay the boundary of the Peak District. Right now, the peaks and geothermal power station were cloaked by a blizzard. Below, the city bustled. Cabs cleaved their way through the whitened corridors and freeways, taking people to restaurants and entertainment or sports centres. Inside, Jade's sound system occupied the whole of one wall. She had taken the edge off the immaculate apartment with her usual clutter.

After listening to one of her latest pieces, Luke said quietly, "You know, somewhere in England right now, someone's killing their partner out of jealousy, their boss in a rage over some gripe, or their neighbour because of greed and envy. Something ordinary like that. I could go in, ask a few questions, take a few samples, and charge a well-known enemy of the victim with murder. All done in a matter of minutes. But I don't get those sorts of cases."

Jade laughed. "Would you be satisfied if you did?"

"Well…"

"People tell me I make challenging music. You've just listened to a case in point…"

"It was brilliant."

"I don't do easy pieces. It's the challenge that makes it fun."

Luke smiled wryly. "Yeah, but murdering people because they're called Emily Wonder! That's… beyond crazy."

Malc interrupted, saying, "Instructor Clint Garrett is trying to contact you urgently."

Surprised, Luke hesitated for a split second. "Sorry, Jade. Put him on the telescreen, Malc."

The instructor's familiar face appeared, larger than life-size on the wall.

"Yes?" Luke said. "Is it something about Emily Wonder?"

Mr Garrett shook his head. "It's another student. Year 7. Name of Tina Stone."

"Yes? What about her?"

"Well, I've just seen the news and it reminded me. She wrote me an essay about a perfect murder weapon. You'll be interested because it was an icicle."

Luke was horrified. "What?"

"Yes. I'm telling you she put in this idea about using an icicle…"

"No," Luke cried. "You said you'd seen it on the news. I haven't released that information!"

"Well, it's just been broadcast nationally a few minutes ago," Clint replied. "Three Emily Wonders dead, one killed by an icicle."

Speaking to himself, Luke muttered, "How did they…?" Looking at the instructor's image again and trying to keep his temper, he said, "Can you download this girl's essay to my mobile?"

"Of course. Anything to help an FI."

"Okay. Thanks. I'll see you – and Tina Stone – as soon as I can."

Once Malc had shut down the link, Luke said, "Find that news bulletin, Malc, and replay it."

Taking the place of Instructor Garrett on the telescreen, the newscaster announced, "It's been revealed that three people with the name of Emily Wonder have been murdered in recent months. Our correspondent has discovered that the deaths, currently under investigation, happened in Dundee, York and Woburn. Extraordinarily, at least one of the women was stabbed to death with an icicle. It is not known if the deaths relate to the opera celebrity with the same name, at present on tour in Lancashire. The singer's spokeswoman declined to comment.

"Scientists monitoring the volcanic island of La Palma in the Canaries are growing increasingly concerned that a huge section of rock on its western side is on the brink of collapse..."

Luke put up his hand and snapped, "That's enough."

Jade looked at him and said, "I think I know what happened."

"Oh?"

"Remember that toddler when we were skating? You nearly chopped him in half, just before you crashed into the icicle. His mother or father probably heard and leaked it to the news."

"Malc?"

"What is your query?"

"You were there. Were they within hearing?"

"Assuming that they have normal human hearing, the father was probably within range, but the mother was not."

"Did I mention the Emily Wonder case?"

Malc hesitated while he located the right sound file in his memory. "Confirmed. In response to the comment that only a warped mind would regard an icicle as a dagger, you said, 'Like the sort of mind that goes around killing people called Emily Wonder?'"

Luke swore.

"What's up?" asked Jade.

"I wanted to keep it quiet. We were the only ones who knew she was stabbed with an icicle so, if a suspect let it slip that he knew as well, that'd make him the killer because Q's the only other person who'd know. But now the whole world's in on it. It's a useless piece of evidence." He sighed and cursed again.

"There is an alternative explanation," Malc said.

"Yeah, I know," Luke replied. He looked at Jade and added, "It'd fit your idea about the motive."

"Oh?"

"If Q wants to terrify anyone called Emily Wonder, it makes sense to advertise his handiwork. Maybe Q told the news people."

"Why don't you ask them?"

"Waste of time. He'll have done it anonymously. Besides, news people never reveal their sources."

Looking on the bright side, Jade said, "At least you've got another lead."

"Mmm. Tina Stone. I'd rather have some decent forensic evidence."

Chapter Thirteen

Barbara Backley's living room was like a desert. The furniture, heating and lighting were designed for the benefit of her collection of cacti, more than the comfort of a human being. "There's fifty-four of them," she told him. "One for each year of my life. Every birthday, my partner treats me to a new one." Near the bedroom door, a large spiky plant, taller than Luke, was reaching for the ceiling. Some were much smaller, but still adopted monstrous shapes. One looked like a mound of hairy green warts. A two-dimensional prickly pear seemed to be topped by rabbit's ears. The fluorescent lightning made the spines of another glow bright red.

"If you live to be a hundred, you'll need a bigger apartment."

Ms Backley did not react. She stared at him severely, waiting.

Luke shivered and said, "I thought cacti liked it hot and sticky."

"In summer, yes, but not this time of year. Dry and cold is best."

Remembering that EW1 had tiny puncture wounds and inflammation on her left arm from a brush with a cactus, Luke headed towards the only one that he knew. In the pot, Barbara had placed a tag that read, *Opuntia vulgaris.* "This is a prickly pear, isn't it?"

Barbara did not appear unsettled. "Yes."

"Can I touch it?"

"Only if you want some needles in your hand and little rash for a while."

Luke withdrew his fingers. "What's so good about cacti? What's the appeal?"

Barbara was clearly surprised that he should ask. "Just look. They're amazing. Tortured shapes. And I think it's something to do with them surviving in extremes. I like the way they cope with water shortage and ferocious heat. Like me coping under stress."

Luke thought it was more likely that they reflected her prickly character. "Have you come across *situs inversus totalis?*"

She frowned. "It means totally the wrong way round, but I don't know what it is. It's not a cactus, if that's what you're thinking."

Luke walked over to the wall-hanging behind the largest cactus and said, "This is nice."

"Yes," Barbara replied warily.

"Clever design." Luke bent down and examined the small label in the lower right-hand corner. *Tartan Textiles, Dundee.* He looked up again and said, "You're a big fan of Emily Wonder, as well as cacti and textiles."

"I know what this is about," Barbara muttered. "Are you really old enough to take charge of a murder case?"

Again and again, Luke faced this question about his age. He realized how maddening it must be for everyone called Emily Wonder always to be asked if they were the opera star. Luckily, Luke had a mobile to answer the tiresome question. "Respond, Malc."

"Forensic Investigator Harding graduated from Birmingham School last year with an unprecedented set of marks. At sixteen years of age, he is exceptionally qualified. This is his third investigation of multiple murder. His success rate is one hundred percent."

Not allowing the concert manager to reply, Luke said, "So, you watched the news yesterday. You heard about the Emily Wonder investigation. Is that what you're saying?"

She nodded. "Emily – the artist – can't be in any danger. She brings so much joy to everyone, no one would want to harm her." She radiated confidence and certainty.

"You regard her as unique."

"She is unique."

"Did you go up to see her perform in York?" Luke asked.

"Yes."

"Dundee?"

"That was a while ago."

"Last July," Luke told her. "You seem to follow her around a lot. How about Woburn?"

"Has she been to Woburn? I don't think I have. It's… a long way away."

"Nowhere near as far as Dundee."

"You know what I mean, Investigator Harding." Barbara turned up her nose. "It's a different culture down there. Not nice. Anyway, I don't like the tone of your questions."

He shrugged. "I'm not a performer. I don't have to please my audience. Now, I'd like to take a look in your kitchen and wardrobe."

"What?" she exclaimed.

"Am I within the law to ask you to scan Ms Backley's clothes and everything in the kitchen, Malc?"

"Confirmed."

Making her annoyance plain, Ms Backley stabbed a finger towards two of the internal doors. "Kitchen. Dressing room."

Luke already had a connection between the concert manager and the first victim: the wall-hanging designed in Dundee. Cacti linked her to the retired gardener, EW3. And she had admitted that she'd been to Dundee and York. He was hoping to find EW2's contact lens or see something in the kitchen that tied Ms Backley to the food technologist but it was a long shot and he soon gave up. Barbara's strongest involvement was with the opera singer and that Emily Wonder was not a victim. Not yet.

"That's all for now," Luke said, emerging from the

kitchen with Malc behind him.

"Good," Barbara replied with a sneer.

"But, before I go, do you happen to know anything about Emily's minder, Freya?"

Barbara shook her head. "Not really. All I know is, Freya Lamacq lives for Emily. She's totally dedicated."

In a way, Barbara Backley was right. Luke did feel too young. He wouldn't admit it but he wished that someone else, someone older and more experienced, was in charge of this thorny case. Inside, a part of him felt that he should still be at school, like many kids of his age, listening to instructors and competing on a sports field. But he had already graduated. The rest of his learning would be conducted in the adult world. He was desperate to complete the case, determined to prove his flair for solving crime, yet he also wanted to be at Jade's side without a care in the world while she gigged in Sheffield nightclubs.

Outside Barbara Backley's quarters, Luke threw up his arms. "I'm torn," he said. "I need to be in Edinburgh, talking to Tina Stone and Clint Garrett, I wouldn't mind having a chat with Freya Lamacq, and I want to be in London, checking out the missing girl."

"Impossible."

"Has she turned up yet, the one in London?"

"No," Malc answered.

"Right, then. That's where I'm headed. As far as I know, Tina Stone's not going anywhere and she isn't in danger. Freya's on tour with Emily, no doubt. Both can wait. A missing Emily Wonder can't. She could be in trouble."

Chapter Fourteen

As Luke neared the southern coast, the temperature increased noticeably. The wind became warmer and less severe, but there were still snowdrifts. The glassy plates of ice over ponds were too fragile to support the weight of skaters but ducks skidded clumsily over them, searching out patches of liquid water.

An ugly reception committee formed as soon as Luke got out of the cab at Greenwich, south of the Thames. Immediately, Malc took up a position in front of him and fired a warning blast at the ground in front of the hostile bandits. The laser beam melted the thin layer of snow instantly, revealing sickly weeds, and burnt them to a crisp. Slowly, the five bandits backed off, grumbling and arguing among themselves. When they were some distance away, they turned and ran.

Watching them retreat, Luke shook his head and sighed. It hadn't taken long for Sheffield to become a distant dream. "Thanks, Malc. Guide me to Greenwich School."

In the shabby staff room, the Principal looked bemused. "Emily Wonder? Now there's a name from the past."

Luke was surprised. "When did she go missing?"

The head of the school let out a long breath as she thought about it. "A year ago? Something like that."

Luke had assumed that it was a recent disappearance. "Was she in trouble? Was there a reason for her to take off?"

"She was... a rascal. Bright girl, but quite a handful. If there was trouble, she'd be in the thick of it but, you know, she never caused it as far as I could tell. More likely she was trying to sort it out. I think she meant well. As rascals go, I liked her. I was sad when she went."

"Have there been any sightings, do you know?"

"No, but..."

"What?"

"If you want to trace her, you should try the old warehouse, past the concrete works. You know where the cabs go into Blackwall Tunnel?"

Luke glanced at Malc and said, "My mobile's got a detailed map."

"You can't go any further without falling in the Thames. It's not frozen so you can't walk across it. Anyway, there's a big round empty warehouse," the Principal said.

"Why there?"

She shrugged. "Just a hunch. A few kids hang out down there, they say. I don't know. It wouldn't be...

clever for me to go. Just watch your step if you check it out."

"Okay," Luke replied. "Thanks."

It was hopeless. The gang of children saw him coming and the floating mobile near his shoulder told them that he was a forensic investigator. By the time that Luke stepped cautiously into the wrecked warehouse, the young people had scattered. There was no one inside. He was saddened by the thought that he might never again rush onto a makeshift pitch and call out, "Over here!" He might never get on the end of a cross and head the perfect goal. His role of FI might always come between him and rogue games.

The empty shelter was filthy and roomy, larger than a baseball ground or football pitch. If Luke had stood at one end and shouted, he was not certain that someone at the other would have heard him.

Luke stood in the middle of the building, drips of water falling steadily from the damaged roof, and said to Malc, "You know what I need to do?"

"No."

"See if you can find an electronic address for Owen Goode, the lad I met in the Lost Bullet case. I need to recruit him."

"You do not have the power to recruit a forensic investigator."

Luke laughed. "I'm not thinking of a formal arrangement, Malc. Just get me Owen."

"Searching."

The white boy surveyed the area carefully, anticipating danger as always. Ready to sprint in the opposite direction if he spotted anything shifty, he lingered in the shadows of North Greenwich cab station for a while. An enormous digger was shovelling stone in the aggregates factory. Next to it, Blackwall Detergents had been shut down for years. He watched Luke Harding and his mobile aid to law and crime for a few minutes before deciding that they were on the level. He broke cover and, scanning from side to side for signs of trouble, walked over to them outside the old warehouse. "Didn't think I'd be seeing you again."

The forensic investigator smiled genuinely and said, "How are you doing, Owen?"

"All right." He wiped his nose on his sleeve.

"Got your own place?"

Owen nodded.

"And a job?"

"Er... sort of."

Luke laughed gently. "I'd better not delve any deeper."

Owen coughed and then sniffed. "Likely you want to use me as bait again. What are you fishing for this time?"

"Nothing dangerous. No bait needed. I'm just trying to find an eleven-year-old girl called Emily Wonder. She's gone missing, maybe in hiding."

Owen was puzzled. "Don't know her. What can I do about it?"

"I... er... I have a certain effect on groups of kids."

Owen smiled. "Yeah. Like, they run away. You want me to be the investigator because they don't run from me."

"Do you know they meet here?" He nodded towards the large dome.

"Yeah. The place is so big, last time I sorted a football match here, it became twenty-a-side or something."

"So," Luke said, "you could ask around for information on Emily Wonder."

"What's she like, this kid?"

"A bit like you, I think. She's got a reputation for being a rascal, but a lovable one."

"Huh." Owen pretended to be hard-nosed but he didn't like the thought of a young girl missing in London. He'd been in the situation himself and he cared for the troublemakers and downtrodden. They were his friends. If he could make this Emily's life safer, he'd do it. "What do I get out of it?"

"A warm glow?" Luke suggested.

"And?"

"I'll tell The Authorities how helpful you've been.

Again. Last time you got an identity card – a passport to a home and goods. This time…" He shrugged.

"Just make sure it doesn't get around that I'm helping an FI. Wouldn't do me any good in places like this."

"You'd be good in a job working with homeless kids, wouldn't you? You're a natural with them. I've seen that."

Owen looked across at a boat on the Thames and thought about it. "Yeah. Not a bad idea."

"I'll talk to The Authorities about you setting up a sort of alternative school in a community centre. Maybe somewhere like this." The FI waved towards the disused warehouse.

"All right. You've got a deal." Owen was thrilled by the suggestion but he didn't show it outwardly. He trusted Luke Harding to do his best, but he didn't trust The Authorities to see the sense in it. He refused to get excited when his expectations lay somewhere between low and non-existent.

"I'll leave you to it. Call me via Malc."

"Yeah. Let someone who knows what he's doing take over. The more an investigator hangs around, the longer it'll take for the kids to come back. Likely, I've got some serious footballing to do before I can talk and get them to open up."

Owen shook his head and smiled while he watched the investigator walk away with his mobile gliding behind him like a faithful pet.

Chapter Fifteen

A tragedy was looming for FI Luke Harding. The pomegranate season was virtually at an end and, unless Malc could find an alternative supply overseas, Luke's breakfasts would have to change. Taking a mouthful of seeds from the fruit and spraying red juice across his room in the Central Hotel, Piccadilly, Luke said, "I'm going to hang around in London till Owen gets back to me – in case I need to go into action on anything he digs up."

Malc replied, "Do you expect him to exhume a body?"

"No. I mean, anything he finds out."

"Information collected by an untrained person is not admissible. I cannot enter it into case notes."

"I didn't get top marks in law for nothing. I know," Luke replied, standing up. "But I'm not sure there's a case yet. If it looks like there is, I'll work on it. Then you'll be able to log things properly." He took a quick shower and then sat opposite the telescreen. "Now, I want a connection with Edinburgh School. Request an interview with Tina Stone."

"You do not have to request it. As an FI, you can demand it."

Luke smiled. "There isn't a law against forensic

investigators being polite, Malc. Request it." He paused before adding, "Firmly, though. I don't want my request turned down."

When Tina Stone entered the telescreen room, she looked nervous.

"Hello," Luke said brightly.

Sitting down, Tina muttered, "Is this a school exercise?"

"No," Luke answered. "But don't worry about it. I read your criminology essay." He raised his arm over his head, his fist clenched around an imaginary icicle, and stabbed it downwards. "Very good. A bit far-fetched maybe, but really clever."

The video image was so clear that the Year-7 student could have been sitting opposite him in his hotel room. She had very short blond hair that clashed with the school's green sweater. She lifted her gaze briefly and dared to look at him – or the likeness of him on the wall in the Edinburgh meeting room. "Thank you." Then she stared down at her own lap again.

"What grade did you get for it?"

Her head still bowed, she smiled. "Starred A."

"I should think so," said Luke. "Where did you get the inspiration for it?"

Tina swallowed before answering. "Outside."

"Outside?"

She nodded. "The cold weather, you know."

Luke could see the silvery top of her head and some of her face. Even without a good view of her eyes, he was not convinced that she was telling the truth. "Did anyone else talk to you about it or did you see it written?"

"No. I just thought it out for myself."

"Are you sure you didn't get the idea from somewhere else? It's okay. I won't tell Mr Garrett. You can keep your starred A."

Tina shook her head and shuffled uneasily in the chair.

She wasn't a suspect. Malc had already downloaded her attendance record for December 23rd and 24th when EW2 died in Woburn. Tina Stone was at the other end of the country at the time. "Do you know Emily Wonder in Year 10?"

"I've heard of her."

"Did you discuss the icicle idea with her?"

"No."

"So, it's just you and Mr Garrett who know about it?"

"That's right."

"Okay. That's all, Tina. You can send him in. Instructor Garrett, that is. Thanks."

As soon as Clint's self-confident face appeared in front of him, Luke said, "Do you know about *situs inversus totalis*?"

The instructor looked puzzled for an instant and then

smiled. "Of course. A classic condition. Rare but classic. They say a man with it escaped death because a well-aimed bullet went through the left of his chest where his heart should've been, but wasn't. I use it as a case study in Year 9." He paused before adding, "Has that got anything to do with Tina?"

"No," Luke answered. "I was just trying to find out how many people know about it. Tina says she dreamed up the icicle plot on her own."

The instructor sat back and thought about it for a few seconds. "She's good, is Tina. Turns in solid B grades and occasional As, so it could be her idea. But she's never strayed far from the humdrum till now. This is quite a leap. I'm going to say it's too imaginative to be Tina's own work."

"You didn't suggest it to her as a subject for her essay, did you?"

"Me?" Mr Garrett uttered, as if taken aback. "No. My job's to train them to think for themselves. I don't come up with ideas for them."

"It wasn't long ago I was at school," Luke replied. "I know how things work. You – the staff – may not know where the idea came from, but some of her fellow students will. She'll have talked about it. I want to see them all – till I find one who's willing to spill the beans."

"That's a lot of…"

"So, we'd better get going, starting with her mates."

It didn't take Luke long to extract the information he wanted. The fourth person he interviewed was Earl Dimmock and he gave the game away almost immediately.

"She's pretty good at criminology. She wants to be an FI like you." Slouching coolly in the chair, he was apparently unruffled by an investigator's questions. "But she nicked that idea from a myth. It was called *Ice Cold*, I think she said."

"Who wrote it? Do you know?"

"No. Wasn't interested. But go online, man, and you'll find it."

"Thanks, Earl. You've been helpful."

"Can I go?"

"Sure."

Invented stories were not very popular but some artists posted their myths online so that people could read them on their telescreens. "Search for a myth called *Ice Cold*, Malc. I fancy a spot of fiction for a change. And I want to know who logged it in the first place."

Luke was getting bored. Fingers interlocked behind his head, he was nearing the end of *Ice Cold*. "I haven't read a story in ages." He pulled a face. "My own cases are weirder than myths. But whoever wrote it got one thing right. The culprit keeps to the same weapon. He starts with an icicle and carries on with an icicle. That's what instructors tell you. Q's getting it wrong. An icicle and a couple of poisons."

"There is a logic," Malc pointed out. "Q is using weapons that do not leave physical evidence."

"Yeah. And I suppose there might be a theme of water. An icicle, probably drinking water poisoned with TTX, and possibly contaminated water in the sauna oil. But they're still different weapons. Anyway, have you found out who posted this myth?"

"Untraceable. It is an anonymous contribution."

"Pity. When did it appear?"

"It was first logged almost five months ago on the fifteenth of August."

"Mmm. Not a very seasonal story at the time."

Malc said, "It is unlikely that Q would broadcast an intended murder weapon online."

"Unless he's into taunting investigators," Luke replied, not yet ready to dismiss *Ice Cold* as a coincidence. "Two jobs for you. Search the database for myths that involve TTX or burning something to make cyanide. If Q's playing games, they'll be there somewhere. Or maybe Q read *Ice Cold* and, like Tina, pinched the idea. So, see if there's a record of computers that have logged on to this myth."

Luke finished off the final paragraphs of the story to prove that he'd worked out the identity of the fictional murderer about halfway through the plot. Other than the icy spikes used as weapons, there was nothing in common with his case. The victims in the myth did not have the same name and none of them were celebrities.

Malc announced, "It is not possible to trace computers that have accessed this or any other myth. The Authorities' central computers do not keep that information on file."

"If I hacked into Edinburgh School's computer…"

"That is illegal."

"Mmm. But if I did, there'd be a list of sites viewed by people in the school."

"Irrelevant, because hacking is illegal."

"I could go back to Edinburgh, present my identity card and get access."

"Confirmed. That is the legal approach."

Luke shook his head. "I don't suppose it'd help much. It'd tell me someone's been reading *Ice Cold*. That'd be Tina Stone. If anyone else in the school had opened it, I wouldn't be able to find out who."

Malc reported his second finding. "The database of myths does not contain any storylines within the parameters that you set."

"All right," Luke said, with a sigh. "This isn't going anywhere. I'm probably barking up the wrong tree."

"That," Malc replied, "would be an unusual activity for a human being."

Chapter Sixteen

The next day, Owen Goode appeared on Luke's telescreen. "Hi. Got your ears pinned back?"

"What?"

Owen paused like someone unused to telescreen messaging and said, "Can you hear me?"

"Yes," Luke replied. "Any luck?"

"Yeah. Your eleven-year-old's been hanging out with that group. For months. But not in the last few days." He sneezed loudly.

"What have you got for me?"

Owen answered, "A little lad. He saw her a couple of weeks back. Something like that. Didn't know when exactly. Every day's the same for these kids. It's not like, double science lesson, it must be Tuesday. Or, no school today, it must be the weekend."

"That'd be just before Year Birth."

"Yeah. Well, that don't mean much to them either. Likely a new year won't bring them any more than the last one. Anyway, this boy saw her walking away with a man. A big man, he said."

"A big man?"

Owen grinned. "I wouldn't rely on it. He's seven. Everyone's big to him. He called me the big man who plays football."

"Did he have any idea about this chap's age?"

Owen shook his head. "Old. Like me – and I'm sixteen."

"Was he touching Emily?"

"How do you mean?"

"Was he dragging her away or was she going willingly?"

Owen shrugged. "Didn't say. But I know these kids. They look after each other. If this bloke was forcing her, they'd be off after him. Likely, she went with him without a fuss."

"Was he smartly dressed?"

Owen smiled again and suppressed another sneeze. "Everyone'd look smart to a lad living rough."

"Okay," Luke said, hiding his disappointment about the man's description. "That gives me something to go on."

"Not a lot, but it's all I got. No one's seen her since."

"Thanks," said Luke. "I put a feeler out to The Authorities about a youth centre and... er..."

"They refused."

Luke nodded. "'Fraid so. Proper students go to proper school. That's it. They didn't really understand the idea."

"You amaze me," Owen replied with sarcasm.

Luke hated the thought that one day he'd get so used to the South's cruelty and crime that he'd accept it as normal. He was scared that he was becoming unshockable. Escaping to Jade and the North for a while wasn't enough. The hopelessness didn't go away when he took a break from it. He wished he could do something to put it right. His idea for an unofficial school would have been one blow in a fight against the seediness of life down South. He was sure that, given the chance, Owen could have lured some kids away from the brutality of crime. "I'll try again," Luke promised.

Owen grimaced. "Won't hold my breath. But…"

"What?"

"I've got this friend. Well, I did, till two years ago. Name of Everton Kohter. He's in prison. Cambridge. He's going to be put to death in a month or something like, but he didn't do the murder. Don't think so anyway."

"We don't make mistakes, Owen."

"Likely you don't, but you're not the only FI."

"The Authorities don't reopen closed cases, if that's what you're asking me to do. They say they get it right first time. Raising doubt doesn't do anything for confidence in the law."

"Seems to me, executing someone who's innocent isn't a clever way of making sure we all trust the system."

"Okay," Luke replied. "I'll do what I can, but…"

"Yeah. I know."

The head and shoulders of an elegant newscaster replaced Owen's white face on Luke's telescreen.

"In the Canary Islands, monitoring of the western side of La Palma continues. A large section of rock remains on the brink of catastrophic collapse. If the volcano does erupt, as scientists expect, a chunk of rock about the size of the Isle of Man will plunge into the Atlantic Ocean and trigger giant swells called tsunamis. Within two hours of the land collapse, waves up to one hundred metres high will wreak havoc on neighbouring Canary Islands and the west coast of Africa. England will not be spared. Four to five hours after the rock breaks off, southern ports will experience ten-metre surges. Some experts warn that waves about twenty metres high will cross the Atlantic and deluge Caribbean islands – and the American and Canadian coast – after nine to twelve hours. Such swells, moving at nearly nine hundred kilometres an hour, will not stop when they strike the coast or a barrier. They are expected to travel inland for ten to fifteen minutes, putting millions of people at risk. Destruction of property is expected to be considerable. Even if the Thames Barrier in London were in working order, it would not hold back a ten-metre tidal wave. Evacuation of the city, the lowlands around the Bristol Channel, and southern ports would be the only option for public safety."

"Sounds grim," Luke muttered. "If it happened, The

Authorities wouldn't be able to evacuate the homeless – the ones without identity cards. It'd be impossible to keep track of people like those kids by the Thames."

"The science of volcanoes is not certain. According to my database, there were warnings about severe landslips in La Palma twelve years ago and three years ago. Volcanic activity subsided in both cases."

"I guess I've got enough on my plate, worrying about forty-four Emily Wonders."

"There is no rational connection between food and your current case."

Luke grinned. "Never mind. Right now, Malc, I want to interview Freya Lamacq. See if you can establish a link. Last time I heard, she was touring in Lancashire."

It took Malc over five minutes to make a connection and, when the singer's minder appeared on the telescreen, she assumed that Luke wanted to speak to Emily. "Ms Wonder can't be disturbed right now," Freya said in a husky voice, almost like a man's. "She's resting."

Luke smiled. "I don't know if you've heard, but an FI can disturb anyone, anytime." Angling for Freya's cooperation, he asked Malc, "Is it true I can demand to speak to her?"

"Confirmed."

Freya began, "I really don't..."

"Look," Luke said, interrupting. "If you think it's a bad idea to fetch her right now, I suppose I could talk to you instead. You'll have to be up front with me, though, or you won't leave me any choice."

Freya jumped at the chance to protect the precious singer. "All right."

"When did you start working for her?"

"As soon as she left school and began to tour."

"What exactly do you do?"

Freya shrugged. "Just about everything, apart from the singing. I make sure we get from one performance to another. I network with concert hall managers, deal with fans, book hotels, handle the media, anything."

"You go everywhere with her."

"True. We're a team."

"It seems to me you're devoting your life to Emily."

"I can think of worse careers, Investigator Harding."

"You're Emily's spokeswoman as well?"

"True."

"Did you contact the media about the news item on three women called Emily Wonder dying?"

"No," she answered. "They called me. I'm well known to them."

"What do you think about it?"

"About what?"

"Are you worried for your Emily?"

"I've organized a private bodyguard," she replied.

"Has any sort of threat come her way?"

"It's hard to see why anyone would do that. No."

Luke watched her carefully as he asked, "Have you ever eaten fugu?"

There was not a flicker as she answered, "I'm not sure what it is."

"Where were you just before the Year Birth Concert? End of December."

"Emily took a break before the recital in Sheffield."

"Where were you?"

"Me?" She seemed surprised that Luke was taking an interest in her. "I…er… I've got friends in Birmingham. I visited them."

"Did you go further south than Birmingham?"

"No."

"I'll need a list of your friends and when you were with them."

Freya's face froze. "What are you accusing me of?"

"Nothing. I'm just checking where all the players were when one of the deaths happened. Where was Emily before the concert?"

"Sheffield's her home city. That's why the performance was so important to her. That, and the fact it was Year Birth. She stayed in Sheffield."

"Do either of you read myths?"

"Emily relaxes by reading them sometimes."

"What about you?"

"Me? No."

Luke thought about it for a moment. "I could catch

up with you, take a look at your computer's log to see which myths she's opened, or I could wake her up and ask her in person right now. Either way, it'd be easier for you to download the list to my mobile."

"What's that got to do with these poor women called Emily Wonder? They're just silly myths."

"Yes," Luke replied. "It's so trivial, you won't mind sending me the details."

Freya sighed heavily. "All right."

Luke regarded Freya as somewhat sinister. He couldn't put his finger on exactly what made him feel that way, but it was something to do with her relationship with the opera star. She hardly seemed to function independently, without the singer. She reminded him of a parasite living on a host and sucking its lifeblood to survive. But he had no idea why she would want to murder Emily Wonder's namesakes.

"Do you know what *situs inversus totalis* is?"

Freya shook her head. "Doesn't sound like the title of a myth."

"That's all for now but I want you to send my mobile a message at the faintest whiff of a threat to Emily."

"I can promise you that, Investigator Harding."

As soon as Malc broke the connection, Luke said, "I can think of two people – Freya Lamacq and Barbara Backley – who adore Emily the opera star. And there's Cornelius Prichard, obsessed with EW1. Does this sort of passion ever get out of hand, Malc?"

"Yes. Studies show that one percent of people who take an interest in a celebrity are suffering from celebrity worship syndrome. Such obsessives, or stalkers, are prepared to harm themselves or others in the name of their idol. They are fascinated by every detail of their chosen celebrity's life, they believe the celebrity is their special friend, and they are prepared to commit crimes on behalf of the celebrity."

Luke nodded slowly. "Celebrity worship syndrome. Interesting."

Chapter Seventeen

Checking with Freya Lamacq's friends in the Midlands, Luke confirmed that she had been in Birmingham on December 23rd and 24th, but he was not convinced that she had a watertight alibi. By fast cab, it was a quick and easy journey from Birmingham to Woburn and there were two gaps in Freya's schedule when she could have made a trip.

Luke's heart rate accelerated when Malc announced, "I have received the the list of myths from Freya Lamacq. It includes *Ice Cold*."

"So," Luke replied, "if our superstar singer wanted to kill off every other Emily Wonder – making her really unique – she might have taken the icicle idea from the myth and asked someone with celebrity worship syndrome – maybe like Freya Lamacq or Barbara Backley – to do the deed for her."

"Speculation."

"So where do I go for hard evidence?" Luke jumped up and brushed back his hair with both hands. "I want to know who grabbed Emily from Greenwich." Putting on his fleece, he said, "I'm going back to her school. What's the best way of getting there?"

"It depends what you mean by best. Do you mean the fastest method or the safest or…"

Impatiently, Luke replied, "Walking would take ages, cabs will struggle to get through. What about the Thames?"

"It is relatively risk-free to walk to Westminster and call a river cruiser from there."

"Right. I want to figure out if Greenwich Emily shares anything with the Wonders who're dead — apart from the obvious. I mean, why those particular three? If the London one's the same, she's up the creek. She may even be dead already." Luke took a deep breath as he sped down the stairs. "I'd rather find her before she becomes EW4."

Luke did not have to ask why children like Greenwich Emily ran away from school. He had only to witness the way of life in the South to see the answer for himself. To some kids, learning a trade must seem like a waste of time. The sooner they were out on their own, the sooner they could learn to fend for themselves in a free-for-all society. They were disillusioned with school, The Authorities, rules, and the prospect of finding a worthwhile job.

Emily did not have a room at the school any more. Her quarters had been given to another student. But the school had kept her possessions. The caretaker had put them in an out-of-the-way locker.

Luke pulled on a pair of latex gloves before he went through the sad pile of her belongings. The first item surprised him. It was a photograph of Emily when she was young, standing between her parents. Luke was taken aback because few people kept family souvenirs. "That reminds me," Luke said to Malc. "Request the most recent picture of her from the school. Download it. I might need it later." Turning back to the drab locker, there were several computer memory cards that probably contained copies of Emily's schoolwork, a few music disks, lots of clothes, and a hairbrush.

Looking closely at the brush, Luke froze. For a moment, he couldn't speak while his mind churned over a new angle. Then he murmured, "It's obvious, but I've been ignoring it!" He held out the brush towards Malc. "Look. There's a couple of hairs. Probably some skin as well. You could get her DNA from this."

"Correct."

Luke was annoyed with himself. The family photograph and strands of hair had seeded an idea that he should have come up with ages ago. "I've been thinking of EW1 to 3 as victims with the same name, but I should've been asking if they're related. I know family isn't a big thing but maybe it is for Q. It is for Emily the IT instructor in Bristol." Blaming himself, he made a tutting noise with his tongue. "You've got DNA profiles from the three victims, haven't you, Malc?"

"Confirmed. It is standard procedure for all post-mortems."

"Can you compare them with each other and with the DNA in the roots of these hairs?"

"Yes."

"Won't that tell me if they've got an ancestor in common?"

"I am not equipped with the necessary software…"

At once, Luke said, "You'd better download it, then."

"Searching The Authorities' files for the programmes."

"When you get them, will the test work?"

"In theory. It is called kinship DNA searching and analysis. One person will have the same genetic markers as close relatives such as parents, brother or sister. An individual will have fewer markers in common with more distant relations like uncles, aunts and grandparents, but will still share some patterns because of the way that humans inherit genes from previous generations."

"Good."

"I have located software that will allow me to explore relationships between individuals from their DNA profiles. I am installing. It will take seven minutes and forty-two seconds."

"Is it accepted in law?" asked Luke.

"That depends on the statistical significance of the findings. Some genetic markers are very common in the population and therefore not reliable to establish kinships. Others are rare and allow relationships to be established confidently. DNA profiles with few matches would not be legally sound, but profiles that are similar would be acceptable for case notes. The software I am installing includes the standards required by law. Kinship analysis has been used only once before. A DNA sample at a murder scene was found to be similar to that of a fourteen-year-old boy by kinship analysis. The boy's uncle confessed to the murder when questioned."

"Could you check any scientific results by searching family trees? Are there records that go back a good few generations?"

"No."

"Okay. I'm going to have to rely on this kinship DNA searching." He dropped the hairbrush into an evidence bag and sealed it. "Come on. That's it. I want you back at the hotel where you can concentrate on the test."

The small cruiser was still moored to the wharf, just along the river from the seven stumps of the Thames Barrier, poking uselessly out of the water. Luke swiped his identity card through the reader and said, "Westminster Bridge". At once, the attachments fell away automatically. The boat wheeled round and began to motor upstream. In London, riverboats were less likely than cabs to be ambushed by bandits. Also, snow, wild trees and shrubs would not block their way. Luke stood at the prow and watched the land slip past: the warehouse dome on the left, docks on the right.

The cruiser navigated the crazy curves of the snaking river, sometimes heading north, sometimes south, as it chugged past Canary Wharf's tower blocks and Rotherhithe. Most of the large docks and smaller jetties that had once been at the heart of a thriving industry were rusting and empty. The heart had stopped beating long ago. There were several sunken wrecks, only their bridges and masts revealing their positions. The working boats were following the zigzags of the Thames only so that they could make their way to the Midlands and beyond. In the centre of the city, Southwark Bridge and Waterloo Bridge had collapsed. Great chunks of the stone had been dragged to both banks of the Thames to leave safe passage for auto-barges.

Making another sweep to the south, Luke was heading for the Houses of The Authorities. The crumbling Westminster Bridge would probably be next to take an unplanned plunge into the river. The cruiser glided to the jetty under the bridge and engaged the attachments. Luke jumped out and, followed by Malc, made for Birdcage Walkway, Green Common and his hotel in Piccadilly.

Back in his room, Luke lay down on the sofa and listened to Jade's music while Malc carried out the genetic tests, unhindered by fatigue or emotion. They had an ideal partnership, Luke and Malc. One provided inspiration and understanding, the other supplied facts and figures.

After three hours of kinship DNA searching and analysis, Malc turned down the volume of the music and stated the result. "There is a sixty-five percent chance that EW1, EW2, EW3 and the missing Emily Wonder shared a distant relative."

His spine tingling, Luke swung his legs over the side of the settee. He did not allow himself to celebrate a breakthrough, though. "Sixty-five percent," he muttered. "I'd have preferred ninety-five."

"Your preference is irrelevant to the conclusion."

Luke smiled. "Yeah. I'll make do with a sixty-five percent chance that I've got myself a new motive to work with. Not just the same name but the same family. Have you entered it into case notes?"

"Confirmed."

Luke hesitated and then said, "This relative they've got. How distant is distant?"

"There are very few genetic markers in common but one of them is scarce, improving the degree of confidence. Close relatives would have many more of the same markers. Therefore, the findings suggest a common forebear several generations ago."

"All right, Malc. Here's what's next. I want DNA samples from all forty-three Emily Wonders. Get The

Authorities to send out agents again. I want to check if any more of them are related. If they are, they'll need protection. The others might not be in Q's sights." He paused, thinking, before he added, "The first one I want is the instructor in Bristol. If she's got the same DNA markers, I'm in luck because she's already done some family-tree research. She'd be useful. The second one's got to be the celebrity singer."

"Transmitting request."

"Make it a demand this time."

Malc replied dryly, "You can demand to interview suspects and witnesses but you cannot demand from The Authorities. It must be a request."

Luke shook his head. "Okay. Make it urgent and impolite." Then he sighed sadly and said, "You know what this means for the eleven-year-old from Greenwich. She's got a link with the other three victims, so she might well be EW4 – or will be as soon as her body turns up." He picked up the printout of her picture, taken by the school when she was ten. Her smile, straight into the camera, was cheeky, as if she knew something spicy about the photographer. Even if Luke had not been told, he would have guessed from her face that she was mischievous and likeable. "I hope I'm wrong but I'm worried for her."

Malc replied, "You would not be human if it did not affect you."

Luke put down the photo and stared at his mobile in surprise. "It's not like you to be understanding. You even sound sympathetic."

"No. It is a fact about human beings."

With a wry smile on his face, Luke said, "What else have I got on Q now? He's a he, according to Owen's witness who saw him walking away from the warehouse with Emily, and he's been looking into the Wonders' family tree. I already know he can lay his hands on TTX and he's got the hang of *situs inversus totalis*." He paused and then, tapping the photograph, he added, "You know, I fear the worst for Emily, but I'm getting somewhere now. I'm beginning to get a feel for Q. Does the IT instructor in Bristol have a brother, Malc? Is there a Mr Wonder?"

It took Malc a minute to find the answer. "Confirmed. He is a writer."

"Ah. Now we're flying. Maybe he's the *Ice Cold* man. Has he posted any work on-line?"

"He has several pieces available via telescreen."

Luke jumped up. "Bob's your uncle!"

"It is true that his name is Robert, but otherwise you are incorrect."

"That's more like you, Malc. Normal service is resumed."

Chapter Eighteen

"How about this, Malc?" Luke said, fresh enthusiasm in his voice. "You get a known piece of writing by Robert Wonder and compare it, sentence by sentence, word by word, with *Ice Cold*. Can you tell if they were written by the same person from the writing styles?"

"There is a five-point scale of certainty in writing comparison. One: total certainty that the same person wrote the pieces. Two: highly probable, when there is very strong positive evidence or when it is very unlikely that the pieces were written by different people. Three: probable, when evidence is significant but not conclusive. Four: inconclusive. Five: no evidence. Only the first three categories are adequate for trials and they require analysis of handwriting and ink. Data from your suggestion will fall into categories four or five because people can change their writing styles at will or type instead."

"Pity."

"I suggest you ask Robert Wonder if he wrote the *Ice Cold* myth."

"Thanks for telling me my job," Luke replied with a grin. "But people come in a five-point scale of reliability as well. One: always honest and truthful. All the way to five: permanently set to lie and cheat."

"I have not been programmed with this scale."

"That's because I just made it up. Crooks don't tell the truth, Malc. I bet Q's a category five. Still, you're right I've got to speak to Robert Wonder – in case he's Q. Where is he?"

"He lives and works in an artists' commune in Leeds."

"Pretty much in the middle of the four crime scenes." Luke settled himself in front of the telescreen but Malc could not establish a link with the writer. He was not at home. "All right," Luke said, feeling frustrated. "We'll get him tomorrow. For now, start downloading everything you can find out from The Authorities' files about the families of the four Emily Wonders."

There was something wild in Robert Wonder's eyes. To emphasize his untamed nature, his long hair was deliberately messy and his green jumper scruffy. He was powerfully built, broad-shouldered and about thirty years old. He looked puzzled at Luke's intrusion, but remained cool. "Hi. What can I do for you?"

Luke decided to plunge straight in. "Did you write a myth called *Ice Cold*?"

Robert grimaced. "A myth? No. I don't know who told you that. I write serious biographies – the life stories of special people. Great artists, musicians and scientists, the big guns of business, and sporting heroes.

Maybe one day I'll tackle the heroes of forensic investigation."

"Investigators aren't heroes," Luke replied. "We're just people who want to do something about crime."

Robert grinned. "Fantastic. You've just given me my first quote."

"You must have to do a lot of research into families."

"Not really. I'm into individual greatness. That doesn't get passed down in the genes. It's something the determined fight for." He paused before adding, "You want to talk to my sister, Emily. She contacted me. For some reason, she's got it fixed in her mind that family background's important." He shrugged.

"You've worked on scientists, you said. You must've had to get to grips with a lot of science."

"Sure do. I immerse myself in each and every subject. Research is the key. Look. I'm… er… very busy. Is there something I can help you with?"

"TTX."

"Tetrodotoxin," Robert replied. "It's a poison in various marine creatures. You could look it up or consult a biologist. I don't know why you ask me."

"I bet you know where you could get hold of some."

"Yeah, but I wouldn't want to. I'd be petrified of the stuff."

Luke changed tack again. "You must travel around quite a bit, like me, to interview people."

"Telescreens are okay but face-to-face is best. Travelling and meeting interesting people are big perks of my job."

"I'm going to put a picture of a ten-year-old girl on your telescreen. Do you recognize her?" He nodded towards Malc.

Robert squinted at the screen and then shook his head. "Never seen her."

"Okay. It doesn't matter," Luke replied. "I've already talked to your sister. Have you had anything to do with her family obsession?"

He laughed. "No. No time, no inclination."

"Have you been to see her in Bristol?"

"No," Robert answered. "Look. Is this about me or my sister?"

"Both. Have you ever done the biography of a notorious criminal?"

"I'd like to, but it's access to information that's the big problem. Someone like you could help me out. Unless you just work on crimes against literature – like arresting whoever wrote that myth you mentioned."

Luke did not react to the joke. "Who are you working on right now?"

"I'm just finishing Jed Lester."

"The middle-distance runner. Where's he now?"

"Well, that's one of the great things about him. He could be somewhere plush like Manchester or Leeds, but he's gone to Milton Keynes to help train kids. He thinks he'll have a greater impact there than in the north. Emily says she's in Bristol for the same reason."

"Didn't Jed Lester come through Dundee School?"

"Yes."

Suddenly, Luke was keen to finish the interview and instead get information on Robert Wonder from his contacts. That way, he'd have more faith in the answers. Besides, Jed Lester had always been one of Luke's heroes so he relished an excuse to meet him. "Thanks," he said to Robert. "That's all. I'll let you crack on with the biography. I'll read it when you post it online." With the telescreen link broken, Luke turned to Malc and said, "Milton Keynes. Interesting. That's within spitting distance of Woburn."

"I dispute that claim. Even with strong following wind, the human…"

"All right. But if Robert went to Milton Keynes to interview Jed Lester and researched his background in Dundee, that puts him near two of the murder scenes. Come on. It won't take long to go back to Milton Keynes. Get your skates on."

"I do not…"

"I wish I could programme you to understand teasing."

Jed stood, hands on hips, watching four of his young stars rushing away from the track. He shouted after them, "You never run that fast for me!" His breath steamed in the cold air.

"My fault," Luke said, holding out his card, identifying him as FI Harding. "I have that effect on certain kids."

"You haven't come to arrest them, have you? No. Obviously not, or you'd be charging after them. You wouldn't stand a chance of..." He stood back and examined Luke's long legs and his physique. "I don't know, though. You look in pretty good shape. Run a couple of laps with me."

Luke glanced down. "I haven't got the shoes for it."

"Excuses!" Jed muttered. "I'm not the age for it any more, but I don't go on about it." He took off down one of the lanes.

Luke smiled and jogged after him.

Even in his forties, Jed ran like a dream. He seemed to float above the surface of the track. He watched Luke beside him for two hundred metres and then said, "You run easy. You're missing your career."

"I always enjoyed athletics – and lots of sports."

Jed nodded his trademark bald head, streamlined for speed. "I can tell."

Luke's hair streamed out behind him. "Your fifteen-hundred metres record has stood for years. That's brilliant."

"It'll go one day. That's why winning races is what this game's all about. Records don't last but no one can take trophies away from you." As they rounded the bend, Jed said, "You didn't come to get some running practice and hints – or you'd have a tracksuit and trainers. So, what *do* you want?"

They were making ground on a group of ten children bunched on the straight in front of them. In a roped-off lane, a thickset sprinter was practising her starts. Luke said, "I want to ask you about Robert Wonder."

"Ah. Him. Those who can, do. Those who can't, write about it." Jed chuckled to himself. "Don't get me wrong. He's a nice fella. It's just that, being pretty useless at everything, he lives through his subjects."

Luke realized that Jed was testing his strength, raising the pace steadily. Luke was not breathless yet, but the great gulps of cold air made his lungs ache. "Did he come and talk to you?"

"Yes."

"When was that?"

"Last month. Towards the end."

Luke lengthened his stride to keep in touch and eased up on the questions while they overtook the band of youngsters. When they moved back to the inside lane, he said, "I bet he looked you up at Dundee School as well."

"I believe so. Probably turned up all sorts of bad

behaviour. He did that ages ago, when he first started."

"When was that?"

"I don't know exactly. Summer. In the middle of that drought."

"Do you have any connection with York?"

Jed laughed. "Where do you think I laid down that fifteen-hundred record? York Races were always my favourite. Fast track."

"Do you know if Robert went there for more information?"

"He said he wanted to talk to the race organizer."

Malc followed them round the track like a robotic telescreen camera, recording the conversation and the race. Luke was breathing more heavily now. But he was comforted to note that he wasn't the only one. Jed opted for short and rapid gasps. "Just one more question. Is there a London connection?"

Jed answered, "No. Never had much to do with the place. What's he done, my biographer?"

"Oh, probably nothing," Luke replied.

"Just don't arrest him till he's finished my story. It'd be a terrible waste if you put him away before he immortalized me online." Then Jed said, "One more lap. If you finish within twenty metres of me, you've got to drop this silly FI business and take up running, probably eight hundred metres."

Luke laughed. "I can't do that. But I'll try and keep

up with you."

As soon as Luke finished talking, Jed kicked for home.

Making no attempt to hide his fatigue now, Luke took a deep breath and accelerated as much as his tired legs would allow. Normally, his pride would be dented by lagging behind a forty-five year-old man, but this was Jed Lester. Luke didn't mind that the retired champion had opened up a gap, especially because it didn't get any bigger down the back straight. In the home stretch, Jed took a few more strides off him, but Luke wasn't far behind when the famous athlete came to a halt.

Luke pulled up next to Jed and a small group of onlookers clapped the two of them.

Jed looked at Luke and said, "Not bad at all."

"What was that? About ten metres behind?"

Malc interrupted. "Fourteen metres and twelve centimetres."

"No need to be so accurate and honest," Luke muttered between breaths.

Chapter Nineteen

Malc had collected all of the available information on the families of EW1 to the missing EW4, but Luke could not find anything unusual in it. There were no curious deaths, no clear interest in family trees, and no significant diseases apart from the wrong-way-round EW2. If there was a motive for murder lurking in the records, it lay hidden.

One by one, the results of DNA tests on all Emily Wonders were trickling in. Each time a result was transmitted to Malc, he performed a kinship search and analysis. "The information technology instructor in Bristol and the opera singer do not share the same genetic markers as the victims. It is highly unlikely that they are related. So far, the only Emily Wonder who does have those markers is the Year-10 student taking criminology at Edinburgh School."

Luke nodded. "Could be the next victim, then. Request a couple of agents to protect her, Malc. And I'd better speak to her right now."

The unattractive girl was in her quarters rather than in a lesson because her lipodystrophy had got the better of her. Feeling under the weather, she was in a bad mood. After she'd listened to Luke, her temper did not improve. She exclaimed, "Bodyguards! What's the point of that?"

"I would've thought it was obvious. Three related deaths and you're in the same family line. I'm not taking any chances with you..."

"No one would dream of killing me, FI Harding. There's no point. I don't have long to live."

"That didn't save a seventy-eight-year-old Emily Wonder in a nursing home."

Ignoring his remark, she said, "You're not being straight with me."

"Aren't I?"

"You're not trying to protect me. You've got me marked down as a suspect. Your bodyguards'll watch every move I make."

"I've got a list of suspects, yes. You know how it works. But I *am* trying to keep you safe."

"Huh."

Luke guessed that a few questions would not make her any more grouchy and uncooperative, so he pressed ahead. "Do you have a brother or a sister?"

"I *did* have a sister." She stressed the past tense with resentment in her voice.

"I'm sorry... Did she have lipodystrophy as well?"

"Yes. It's very rare, the medics say, but we both inherited it. I think I'm the only one in the country now."

"Have you ever taken an interest in your family background?"

Emily shook her head. "No."

"Do you know if your Biology Department up there has got a collection of marine life?"

"This is Edinburgh School," she snapped. "Of course it does. We're big on oceans, ships, overseas trade, anything watery or fishy. Mr Garrett's particularly keen on that sort of thing."

"Is he? Okay. Thanks. What does he like to do with his weekends?"

"Why don't you ask him? Good investigators don't deal in hearsay. He gets away from school. That's all I know."

"Fair enough. Watch out for your minders. They'll turn up any time soon."

Irritated, Emily snorted noisily.

Malc manoeuvred himself in front of Luke. "I cannot enter her comments about Instructor Clint Garrett into case notes because, as she stated, they are hearsay. However, you should regard him as a suspect."

"Agreed," Luke replied. "EW1 was murdered on a Saturday and EW2 could well have been stabbed on Saturday the 24th of December. I wish I knew when Q planted the poisoned sauna stuff in York but, if I'm looking at a weekend killer, it might mean he can't get away on workdays. Like an instructor."

"Clint Garrett has specialist knowledge of criminal

investigations," Malc pointed out.

"Mmm. Sounds like he's into marine creatures – so he's bound to know about TTX – and we know he marked Tina Stone's essay so he's no stranger to the icicle idea. On top of that, in a sea of Emily Wonders, he's male."

"You need to consider his motive."

"Emily's his pet student. He's obviously upset that genetics dealt her a rotten hand. That means, she was unlucky enough to be born with lipodystrophy. Maybe he's showing related Emily Wonders – the ones who could've inherited it but didn't – what it's like to die early." Luke shrugged. "If that's right, there's no point protecting her with agents. She wouldn't be on his hit list. But I'm not risking it. I might be barking up the wrong tree again and she is a target."

Having entered the informal phrase into his dictionary, this time Malc did not object to Luke's language.

"There's always Robert Wonder," Luke continued. "I can put him at the site of all three murders and he's familiar with TTX. He says he didn't write *Ice Cold* but I can't be sure about that. I don't know about his motive, though. By the way, I can see a motive for Freya Lamacq and Barbara Backley – making their Emily unique – but I don't know why they'd go for Emily Wonders in the same family tree. They'd want to track down and get rid of all her namesakes. It's the same for anyone with celebrity worship syndrome. Anyway, there's a huge problem with them both. It was a man who walked off with the London EW. That stops me putting an Emily Wonder on a list of realistic suspects."

"The man seen by the Greenwich witness may not have been Q."

"I know. But I don't want to think about accomplices without some evidence that there is one. Most murders are solo performances." Luke got to his feet and said, "I can't just sit here thinking and waiting for EW4's body to turn up. I need to get my teeth into some forensic evidence right now."

"Chewing crime-scene artefacts is not…"

"Come on. Time for another river cruise." Luke hesitated before asking with a grin, "That landslip in the Canaries hasn't happened, has it?"

"No."

"It's safe, then. Well, as safe as Greenwich can be. On the way, I'll have another dictionary definition for you – something to get your teeth into."

Chapter Twenty

Walking from the wharf to the disused dome, built in a loop of the Thames, Luke was determined not to scare away the warehouse kids this time. He wanted to approach them without advertising himself as an FI, so he told Malc to stay out of sight.

Malc objected. "It is dangerous for you to be without my protection in London."

"People like Owen Goode seem to stay in one piece without a mobile."

"Owen Goode has been shot and wounded, and Emily Wonder is not safe. In addition," Malc said, "The Authorities require you to follow my advice. They do not approve of your unorthodox methods."

"Okay. Ask your circuits this, Malc. What's happened every time you've come with me to meet kids living rough?"

"They have run away."

Luke nodded. "Right. Now think how I'm going to get some more evidence on the missing girl. People shed ten thousand scraps of skin every minute so whoever took her has left some skin around here somewhere. No question. You could do DNA profiling on a single flake if only we could find it."

"Impractical. There will be millions of skin fragments

from many different human beings."

"Exactly. Frustrating, isn't it? But what's the answer? I could narrow the search by speaking to Owen's seven-year-old witness, but he'll run away if you come with me."

"My programming cannot resolve this dilemma. Your logic is correct but I am under instruction to accompany you at all times on a case."

"Well, you're just going to have to trust me. You hide out of the way. Keep a lookout on the entrance if it makes you happier."

"I do not experience…"

"Yeah. I know. But have we got a deal?"

"I can oversee your safety by keeping the approaches to the building under surveillance from a distance."

"Thanks, Malc. You're a pal."

Luke could see a gang of about thirty children in the vast empty space of the warehouse. He could also see Owen refereeing a game of football. Owen was probably the only one of them who had a home address and an identity card. The others should have been in school. The play stopped for a moment when they noticed Luke but then a girl cried, "Corner!" and the game continued.

In a hoarse voice, Owen shouted, "Carry on for a bit." Then he walked off the improvised pitch towards Luke. "I… er… I came back. They're an okay bunch of kids."

"I'm glad you're here."

Owen glanced around and said, "No mobile. Have they sacked you?"

Luke smiled. "Not yet. Is that seven-year-old around?"

"Yes. Look. They put him in goal. Likely the worst keeper I've ever seen. Far too small."

"I need him for a minute. All right?"

Owen coughed. "It won't be a great loss to the team. I'll go and get him, though. He trusts me."

The boy stood between Owen and Luke on the rough ground outside the old warehouse.

"You know that man who went off with Emily?" Luke said, squatting down in front of him. "Are you sure it was a man?"

The boy avoided Luke's eyes and instead looked up at Owen with an unspoken question on his face.

"As investigators go," Owen said with a smile, "this one's okay."

"Yes. A man," he answered.

"Where did you see them?"

"I was here."

"I mean, where were they?" Luke swept his arm in front of him, indicating the barren landscape from the Thames on his left, past the gaping mouth of the tunnel, the aggregates factory and the derelict building of Blackwall Detergents, to the Thames on his right.

The young lad shut his eyes for a few seconds and then he pointed towards the concrete works. "They was there. They was walking to the river. That way."

"Thanks," Luke replied. "That's helpful. What was the man wearing?"

The boy shrugged. "Don't know, but he'd got a green scarf on."

"Was Emily carrying anything? Like a bag maybe."

He closed his eyes again and screwed up his face, apparently concentrating on a rerun of the scene in his mind. When he opened them, he said, "Yes."

"What sort of bag? What colour?"

"Blue. A rucksack sort of thing."

Owen wiped his nose with a hand. "Likely she had a blanket."

Luke nodded. Speaking to the boy again, he said, "That's great. I'm going to try and find her."

He pulled a face. "Are you going to put her in prison?"

Luke smiled. "No. I'll prove it to you." He stood up and shouted for Malc. While the robot glided to his side, he touched the young lad's arm kindly and said, "Don't worry. You're not in trouble. You know a mobile can't lie, don't you?" Seeing him nod, Luke looked up at Malc and asked, "Am I trying to arrest Emily Wonder?"

"No."

The boy flinched away from Malc but seemed satisfied that Luke was on the level.

"I want to get her back here if I can – so she can carry

on with her life. Right now, though, I want you back in goal. I hope your team hasn't let any in because I dragged you away. Thanks."

The tiny goalkeeper did not need a second invitation. He turned and ran back inside as quickly as he could.

"Good work," Luke said to Owen, nodding towards the game inside.

"Good luck," Owen replied with a impish grin. "You'll need it."

Luke took Malc to the huge gate leading into the aggregates firm. "This is where they started, Emily and the chap who abducted her. They walked east towards the Thames. Scan for anything and everything, Malc, but we're looking for a blue rucksack."

"There is too much debris to analyse individual particles like skin. It is beyond my capabilities."

"Just scan and record. If we spot anything worthwhile – like her bag – you can do detailed tests on it. If the mystery man touched it, you might be able to get a print or a bit of skin. That's the idea."

Keeping his eye on the ground in front and to each side, Luke walked slowly towards the river, looking for anything that might be significant. Going past a tall wooden fence, he asked Malc, "What's on the other side of that?" He imagined that someone could have thrown a bag over it and out of sight.

Malc zoomed upwards and directed his sensors into the

enclosed yard. "It is a builder's storage area. It appears to be deserted and I do not detect any relevant items."

"Thanks." Luke leaned against the fence and said, "Just a minute." He yanked off his right boot, tipped it upside down and watched two sharp pieces of aggregate fall out. "I don't know how it gets in, but it always does. It's a pain."

"Smaller particles will adhere to the lining," Malc told him.

"As long as they don't hurt," Luke replied, slipping his boot back on. He resumed the walk while Malc hovered near his shoulder.

Two cabs rushed past each other in opposite directions. Blackwall tunnel swallowed one and released another at the same time.

Luke paused and asked, "Can you go in the tunnel, Malc, and scan around?"

"No. It is forbidden for any mobile aid to law and crime to enter. I could cause an accident, harming travellers or myself."

"If Q's hot on criminology, he'll know that," Luke pointed out. "It's an ideal place to hide something – like a bag or a girl's body."

"To gain access, you would have to make a request to The Authorities and, if granted, they would temporarily disconnect the power to the tunnel."

"I'll carry on for now. Maybe later."

Luke was getting more and more desperate as he neared the Thames. He was not far from the quay where he would call a river cruiser to take him back to the hotel. By now, he realized, he could be well away from the route taken by Emily Wonder and the unknown man.

He leaned on the rail at the riverbank. Two metres below him, the Thames slapped the muddy shore lazily. To the north, there was a ramshackle jetty. Attached to the waterfront by rusty scaffolding, it was floating at a crazy angle. On the pontoon there was a silo with a chubby seagull sitting on top. Further back from the bank, a tower crane stood silently, stretching its neck towards the darkening sky. Once, the giant had swung its horizontal arm to and fro, loading and unloading cargo from ships. Luke doubted that it would ever move again.

Malc commented, "If someone living falls in the Thames, the shock of the cold water will paralyse the limbs almost at once and the body will sink. Eventually, the body will resurface. This U-bend is a trapping point for bodies, no matter where they entered the river."

Luke sighed and looked south towards the wharf. At once, he pointed to the frame that supported it. "Look!" In the river, caught around one of the tarred wooden posts, something blue bobbed up and down. He ran towards the quayside, shouting, "Use a water-penetrating scan, Malc. There isn't a girl under it, is there?"

Chapter Twenty-One

Luke found a long wooden pole fastened to the wall of the boathouse. It had a steel hook attached to one end and it had probably once been used to grab boats and drag them to dry land. Luke grasped it in both hands and took it to a point on the walkway that was closest to the rucksack. He leaned over the railing and stretched downwards with the rod. Malc had made sure that Emily Wonder was not under the bag so Luke could lift it out of the Thames without disturbing a murder scene.

At his third attempt, he got the hook around one of the straps but, when he pulled on the pole, the backpack would not budge. "The other strap must've caught round something," he muttered, yanking again without success. Making sure that he kept the shoulder strap hooked, he walked along the rail so that he could tug on the bag from a different angle, like a fisherman who had snagged his line. This time, when he jerked the pole, the blue rucksack flew up. "Got it!"

He landed his catch without touching it and laid it on the concrete jetty, as if it were an exhausted fish. His excitement soon gave way to a long weary sigh. "So much for getting a bit of Q's skin or a hair off it. Or a fingerprint. Everything will have been washed away. That's probably why he threw it in the Thames. Oh well.

Here goes."

While he pulled on his gloves, a small pool of water formed around the backpack and Malc scanned its exposed surfaces.

"Anything?" Luke asked.

"Yes. Contamination from the river."

"Great." Luke turned it over so that Malc could examine its back.

Within seconds, his mobile reported, "There is a short green thread caught in the left buckle."

"Green," he repeated. "Like the man's scarf." He felt a prickling down his back. "Maybe he stood here somewhere and gave the bag a good swing to chuck it in the water. It could have brushed against his scarf on the way." Luke mimicked the action and then smiled. "Yeah. That's possible. One fibre's not much, but it's better than nothing. A lot better. And green's the colour you see all the time at Edinburgh School. Come on. Back to the hotel. I want you to analyse it chemically, and I want to open the bag and see what's inside."

Before the cruiser spun round and headed back towards Westminster, Luke looked downstream. At once he felt glum again. He was wondering if Emily was out there somewhere. If she'd drowned and her body had not become snagged like the rucksack, it could have drifted out to the open sea. If that had happened, it could be months before the tide deposited her remains on a beach. Worse, she might never be found.

But she could still be alive. Luke felt a great sympathy towards her. He was always drawn to loveable rogues. He was desperate to give her back her life, if he could. What's more, she could help him. She could identify the man who had snatched her.

The contents of Emily's backpack did not tell Luke anything about Q – if it was Q who had abducted her – but they told him a lot about her sad and simple life. The bag contained two very soggy blankets, a spare set of clothes, and a furry toy. Under the cute cat, there was a mush that had once been bread. These seemed to be her only belongings.

Luke had not expected to find evidence of Q inside the rucksack but he still shook his head miserably. He was touched by Emily's pitiful possessions. "Nothing here," he said to Malc, trying to keep focused on the investigation. "What have you got?"

"Explain your enquiry."

"Have you analysed that green thread?"

"Confirmed."

"And what's the result?"

"The infrared spectrum has the distinctive pattern of a synthetic acrylic fibre. Specifically, it is Acrilan, often used as a substitute for wool."

"I need to go to Edinburgh School and check it

against green fibres there."

"That would be valid and beneficial. To aid future comparisons, I have also recorded the visible spectrum of the green dye but this may have been affected by exposure to water."

"There's something else. What do you get if you burn Acrilan?"

"Under most conditions, carbon dioxide, water and hydrogen cyanide."

Luke nodded. "Cyanide. Thought so."

Forensic Investigator Harding went to sleep in a lowly southern city and woke up alongside the plush Princes Freeway. As always, Malc had stayed alert for the entire journey but he had taken the opportunity to recharge his batteries from the wind-farm supply as they'd sped north. Getting out of the cab, Luke stood still and stretched in the chilly morning, appreciating the centre of Edinburgh. It was as if he'd woken in a totally different world – the opposite of London. The homes, businesses and suppliers in the main freeway were neat and stylish. And they were topped with a thicker layer of snow than buildings in the south.

"I'll walk to the school," Luke announced. "I could use some fresh air and exercise." He took a deep breath and then added, "I'll call in somewhere that'll give me a pomegranate breakfast with a bit of luck, and a shower.

Then I'll catch Clint Garrett before he does anything with his weekend." Luke felt good. He had a meagre amount of forensic data but he was confident that even a single fibre would point him in the right direction. He just needed to find a match.

He intercepted the criminology instructor as he was about to leave his quarters in school. "Good morning," Luke said brightly.

"Oh… Hello. I didn't expect… You'd better come in. What can I do for you? I haven't got long, though."

"Let's get on with it, then. Do you have a green scarf?"

"Of course. A school scarf."

"I need to see it – and take a couple of threads from it."

"What?" he exclaimed.

"I want to test its fibres."

Clint looked angry. "I can't stop you but you're making a terrible mistake. Besides, just about everyone here's got a school scarf and, in case you haven't noticed, all the students have got green uniforms."

"Fetch the scarf for me, please."

Mr Garrett disappeared into his bedroom and Luke heard the sound of a drawer opening and closing. The instructor returned with the scarf draped over his arm.

Luke placed a clean polythene bag on the table and then pushed some sticky tape against the scarf to remove a few fibres. He placed the tape on the spotless surface and asked Malc to perform a microscopic examination, and infrared and visible spectroscopy to identify the thread and define its colour.

"I hope you agree I'm doing this properly," he said to Clint, "but you haven't asked me why. Strange. Perhaps you know."

"It's not strange. I don't need to ask. You must've found a green fibre at the scene of one of your murders. But I'm going to tell you it's got nothing to do with me."

"Well, it doesn't sound as if you've got anything to worry about, then. Any second now, Malc's going to prove you're innocent." Luke barely hesitated. "What do you normally do at weekends?"

"I get away. I go walking. That's what I'd planned… Hill walking. It's a hobby. It clears away the cobwebs of working all week."

"Is that on your own?"

"Yes."

"So, there's no one to confirm where you were on Saturday the 16th of July and the 24th December."

"You can't expect me to remember those particular weekends but, no, there's no one to vouch for me."

Malc broke into the interview to announce, "The scarf is made of Acrilan. The green dye and diameter of the textile fibre are identical to the thread found in the Thames, taking into account some slight weathering."

"Interesting," Luke said. "It's not looking good for

you, Mr Garrett. I've got to bring a team in to search your apartment. Every square millimetre."

"But…" Clint spluttered.

"Yes, it'll be messy and disruptive. If Malc scans around now, it'll save you quite a bit of the mess. You see, I want to check your winter coats, trousers and shoes. I'm not going in your bedroom in case I contaminate it, but you could open everything and get your shoes out, so my mobile can do some tests. If you're innocent as you say…" He shrugged. "I can't see why you'd object or try to hide anything."

"All right," Garrett snapped. It was probably anger rather than embarrassment that made his cheeks glow red. He marched back into his bedroom and opened his wardrobe door so that Malc could scan the coats and trousers inside. Then he extracted his shoes from under a chair.

"Put them upside down on the floor," Luke said from the doorway, "so Malc can analyse what's on the soles. Right. Thanks. Let's leave him to it."

Back in the living room, Clint fell into a chair.

Luke asked, "Ever eaten fugu?"

Clint's face crinkled into confusion. "What's that got to do with anything?"

"Have you?"

"As a matter of fact, yes."

"Risky."

Mr Garrett denied it. "Not in the hands of a good chef who knows how to prepare it properly."

"Some people still get TTX poisoning and die."

"I'm still alive, aren't I?" Clint muttered.

"Can you get pufferfish round here, then?"

"Yes. If you know the right place to go."

"I heard you were into marine life."

He nodded cagily.

Suddenly it dawned on Luke that Clint could be holding back. "Are you qualified to cook puffer by any chance?"

"It's a little hobby of mine. Yes, I am actually."

Luke smiled to himself and changed tack. "How many scarves have you got?"

Mr Garrett shrugged. "Four, I think."

"All green?"

"No. Only one."

"What do you really think of Emily Wonder – your favourite criminology student?"

Garrett sat upright with a jolt. "She's all right, isn't she? She hasn't…"

"As far as I know, she's fine," Luke said.

"I feel enormously sorry for her. Nature's not fair."

"Have you been trying to make up for that?"

Again, Clint looked puzzled. "I don't know what you…"

He was interrupted by Malc who glided into the

room and announced, "I have not completed the scan yet, but there is a highly significant find."

"What's that?" Luke asked eagerly.

"At the bottom of the wardrobe, there is a contact lens that matches the prescription for EW2."

Chapter Twenty-Two

"If you can't explain what the contact lens is doing in your wardrobe, you're in deep trouble," Luke told the instructor.

Clint Garrett shook his head helplessly, lost for words.

"Do you wear contact lenses?"

"No."

"The second victim did, and one of hers went missing. Now it looks like it's turned up in your apartment." Luke hesitated before asking, "How do you explain that?"

"I... I don't. I can't."

Luke stared at him. "If you were me, what would you make of it?"

Garrett was speechless again. He merely shook his drooping head.

"All right. I'm suspending this interview until my mobile's finished. I want him in here to record video as well as sound."

Malc made a second find that added to the case against Clint Garrett. A few concrete chips had lodged in the tread of one pair of his shoes. "Concrete is made of cement and aggregate – gravel or sand usually," Malc explained. "Almost all of the concrete in Edinburgh uses beach sand. All the grains have similar dimensions because waves separate the sand by size. The grains also show microscopic triangular marks where waves have pounded sharp sand particles onto their faces. Several samples adhering to the soles of Mr Garrett's shoes do not bear scratch marks and consist of a mixture of very different grain sizes. They are not typical for Edinburgh. They match the aggregate extracted in North Greenwich. Chemical analysis will identify the source rock and confirm or deny the match."

Luke reached down and yanked off one of his own boots. "I walked through lots of the stuff the other day. Is there any on mine?"

"Confirmed."

"Compare and contrast, please, Malc."

Letting Mr Garrett stew for a while, Luke sat in silence. He should have been tingling with pleasure. He should have been celebrating internally. All of the pieces were falling effortlessly into place. It was like the moment when he solved a school exercise. And that was what was bothering him. Somehow, it was too neat. The real world was much messier than a school project.

Clint Garrett barely looked up. Distraught, he buried his face in his cupped hands and murmured, "I don't believe it. This can't be happening." Damp patches of sweat had begun to appear on his shirt.

Keeping his eyes on Mr Garrett, Luke produced the

photograph of the missing girl and asked, "Do you recognize her?"

The instructor looked at the likeness and shook his head. "No."

Malc came back into the living room and delivered his verdict. "The ratio of the minerals zircon and staurolite is identical. The aggregate on Instructor Garrett's shoes is the same as that on FI Harding's."

Luke looked piercingly at Clint. "That means your shoes have been in North Greenwich recently."

"I can't... This isn't happening to me."

Speaking to his mobile, Luke said, "Were there any fingerprints on the shoes?"

"Confirmed. Only one partial print does not belong to Mr Garrett. It is not in my database." Then Malc added, "There is sufficient evidence to charge Instructor Clint Garrett with the murder of Emily Wonder in Woburn and the abduction of a different Emily Wonder in London."

Astonished, Mr Garrett stared open-mouthed at the robot.

Luke did not react straightaway. He sniffed and thought about his next move. Then he shook his head and said, "No."

"The Authorities require you to arrest and charge this suspect."

Instructor Garrett could have been on the edge of his

seat at a tennis match. He gazed in anguish at Malc, and then turned towards Luke before glancing back at Malc. He seemed to be willing Luke to win the contest.

"Mmm. But I've made my decision." Talking to Garrett, Luke said, "I want your identity card. I'll get the school secretary to downgrade it so it can't be used outside. That's it. For now, I'm not arresting or charging you, but I'm confining you to the premises."

"I... Thank you."

Luke held out his palm until the instructor handed over his identity card. Pausing on the way to the door, Luke asked, "By the way, is there anyone in school who'd like to see the back of you?"

Clint gawped at Luke for a moment before the bewilderment lifted from his face. "You mean, is someone trying to frame me? Yes, that's it!" he said, clutching at the straw. "You're right. I'll tell you this. I've had quite a few arguments with Earl Dimmock over the years. He's one of Tina Stone's friends. Well, hardly a friend. Sometimes they get on, other times they're at each other's throats. You spoke to him about icicles, remember?"

Luke nodded.

"It'll be him."

If a machine could get annoyed, Malc would have fumed. "You should have charged Clint Garrett with murder and abduction."

"I know, but..." Luke shook his head. "Get your electrons around this. It's too easy. He's got four scarves. If he was planning to kill EW4, would he really wear the one that points to Edinburgh School? And that contact lens lying at the bottom of a wardrobe as if it's fallen off one of his coats. It's just too convenient. I smell a rat."

"You are incorrect. There are no odour components indicative of vermin."

Luke did not stop to explain. "Even though everything points at him, I'm not sure. Would he have called me about Tina Stone's icicle story if he's the one who used it? I think he's genuinely shocked. And I could tell by the look on his face he really didn't recognize EW4's picture." On the way to the secretary's office, Luke lapsed into silence while two students in school uniform walked past them. "The green thread could have been a deliberate plant but, even if it wasn't, everyone here's in green – like the two that just came past."

"Some of those garments are cotton," Malc replied. "The colour matches but the infrared signature of the material is entirely different."

"Garrett's not going anywhere. If he's guilty, I'll arrest him later. Right now, I want to see Earl Dimmock. I reckon he could fall into the category of a big man through the eyes of a seven-year-old."

Luke got Earl out of a lesson in politics and took him to an empty common room.

Flopping casually into a chair, Earl said, "Hey. Did you get anywhere with that *Ice Cold* myth – if I remembered its name right?"

Amazed at the boy's coolness, Luke replied, "Yeah. And you got the title spot on. You didn't write it, did you?"

The student laughed. "Check out my English marks, man. They're negative."

"That is incorrect," Malc stated.

Earl laughed even louder. "You've got my school records! Well, writing isn't me. I'm a stranger to grades over D in English."

Luke liked this boy, but he tried to put aside his feelings. After all, it was possible that Earl was a calculating multiple murderer. "Malc, check Earl's attendance records for Saturday 16th of July and 24th December."

Earl creased his brow but remained relaxed, as if he'd got nothing to worry about.

After a few seconds, Malc answered, "Earl Dimmock was not in school during those weekends."

"What's going on?" Earl asked.

"Just tell me where you were," Luke replied.

"I doubt if you'll believe me, but I visit my family."

"Your family? You mean, your parents? You keep in touch?"

"My mother and father like to hear what I'm getting up to at school."

Luke said, "Do you look into family trees? Are you into that sort of thing?"

"No. It's not like you think. It's just that I get on well with them. My parents, that is."

"Where are they?"

"Here in Edinburgh."

"If I contact them, will they confirm your visits?"

Earl grinned at him. "I don't see why not. It's unusual, I know, but it's not illegal."

"No. I think it's... nice."

Malc interrupted to say, "Under these circumstances, testimony from parents would be unreliable and inadmissible."

"Yeah, but... Earl, give me the contact details anyway in case I want to talk to them by telescreen."

Earl shrugged and recited their electronic address for Malc's benefit. Then he asked innocently, "What am I supposed to have done? I know you're interested in Tina and her icicle murder. That's all. Word going round is you're on the Emily Wonder case."

"True."

"That's got nothing to do with me. Do you know we've got an Emily Wonder in Year 10?"

"Yes. I know all about her."

"She's the peculiar-looking one. Even taller than you."

Luke was about to respond but caught his breath. A shiver started at the back of his neck and ran down his spine. "Thanks, Earl. That's all. You've been helpful. Again. I've got to get on."

Clearly surprised at the sudden shift, Earl said, "Oh. Okay. Can I go?"

"Sure."

Chapter Twenty-Three

Out of habit, Emily played with the long and bony fingers of her left hand. Her stern face, thrown out of balance by her outsized chin, looked pale and sickly. The disease had taken a tighter grip on her since Luke last saw her in person. Lipodystrophy seemed to be draining her remaining strength and resistance. Slowly, Luke prowled right around her, trying to keep in check his natural sympathy that threatened to blind him to her true nature. From the back and side, she could easily have been mistaken for a man. Her height added to the masculine impression.

"You said you hadn't looked into your family tree," Luke remarked. "My mobile's going to log on to your computer and see if its records agree."

Emily shrugged her scrawny shoulders. "Feel free."

While two agents lurked outside the student's quarters, Malc interrogated her computer and then announced, "This is a new disk drive. There is very little history to examine."

Luke sat down opposite her and smiled. "What a coincidence. What happened to your last hard drive?"

"It developed a fault. I had to scrap it."

Turning towards the robot, Luke said, "So, there's no reference to the *Ice Cold* myth either?"

"Correct," Malc answered.

Emily shook her head with a tired grin. "I don't know why you're here, making a nuisance of yourself when I'm feeling down. You haven't got a scrap of evidence against me." She faced Malc and asked, "Has he?"

Malc replied, "I respond only to FI Harding."

"He'll scan your apartment now," Luke said, ignoring her comment. "And your fingerprints."

Luke used the same procedure that had worked in Clint Garrett's quarters. He got Emily to open her wardrobe and drawers and lay out all of her shoes and the only scarf that she owned. "Use your finest search, Malc," he instructed. "Scan absolutely everything. Shoes, boots, coats, socks, gloves, the lot. Then scan the wardrobe and the rest of the room. I don't care how long it takes. And while you're doing it, record what we're saying in the living room."

"Processing."

Sitting down again, Luke decided to provoke her. "You're wrong about evidence. You were seen in Greenwich, walking off with your namesake. I've got a witness."

For the first time, a crack appeared in her defences for a fraction of a second. Then she laughed. "That's evidence, is it? Someone *thinks* they saw me – walking away with a girl called Emily Wonder. Even if it was me, walking's not the same as murdering or kidnapping.

Check your school notes. All that proves is someone who looks like me took a stroll with one of your victims."

"Why did you call her a girl?"

"What? Did I?"

"You said, 'A girl called Emily Wonder.'"

"What else could she be?" the criminology student asked.

"She could have been an old lady. I didn't say anything about her age."

"I just assumed, I suppose."

"Where is she, Emily? What did you do to her?"

"Why would I want to do anything to her – or anyone else with my name?"

"They were part of your family tree, stretching way back, but none of them got lipodystrophy. Only you and your sister. Unlucky. You're cut up about it, so you gave them a taste of what it's like to die too soon. Knowing what you do about investigations, though, you killed them with weapons that don't leave a trace. So, what did you use in Greenwich? Potassium chloride or air injected into an artery to stop the heart? An injection inside the mouth was your suggestion. Or have you locked her away without water or food – or air?"

"I don't know what you're talking about, Investigator Harding."

"I've also got a green thread that'll match your scarf."

"So, you've found…" She hesitated and then continued, "A fibre. Congratulations. That narrows it down to a couple of thousand kids in school. Except there's bound to be more schools with the same uniform."

Luke was sure she'd been about to blurt out that he'd found EW's rucksack. If she had, he would have charged her with abduction because only the culprit would know about the backpack. "It turned up in a Greenwich warehouse," Luke lied.

The flicker of surprise on her face would mean nothing in a trial. It would not have impressed Malc if he'd captured it on video, but it meant a lot to Luke. It told him that she knew the bag had not been dumped in the dome. It told him that she was Q.

"So?" she said, staring harshly at him.

"Why look shocked?"

"Did I?"

"Mmm. As if you didn't expect the thread to turn up in a warehouse."

"No," she replied. "Just that I didn't expect you to tell me where you found it at all."

Keeping his eye on Emily's face, he shouted towards the bedroom, "Update, please, Malc. How's it going?"

"There are many fingerprints that match the partial print on Instructor Garrett's shoe, but I have not found any significant traces. Several items of clothing, including a fleece coat and the school scarf, have been laundered recently and one pair of boots has been cleaned very thoroughly."

Luke thought about it and then smiled. "The boots, Malc. Use your laser to split them open, then scan the inside."

"No!" Emily cried.

"What's the problem?" asked Luke.

"You can't just…"

"I can. You know Malc would've objected if it wasn't allowed in law."

"It's just that… They're my favourite."

"Sorry," Luke said, as the faint smell of burning leather wafted into the living room. "But that's not what's worrying you. It's easy to clean the outside, isn't it? Not so easy to get everything out of the inside. Who knows what might've dropped down and got caught in the lining." Luke paused for a few seconds before asking, "Why is your fingerprint on a pair of Mr Garrett's shoes?"

She shrugged. "Maybe I touched them in class. Maybe when I dropped something on the floor in front of him."

"Not very convincing," Luke remarked. "Have you heard of *situs inversus totalis*?"

"No," she snapped.

"Well, that's funny because Mr Garrett told me he used it in a Year-9 exercise."

Rattled, she replied, "Oh, yes. I remember now."

"You denied it because you don't want me to know you researched your family and turned up the fact that Emily Wonder in Woburn had it. That's how come you knew where to stab her."

"I forgot the lesson. That's all. A lot of what Mr Garrett says isn't very memorable."

Luke nodded. "You don't like him much, even though he thinks a lot of you. Is that why? Is he trying too hard to sympathize? Sometimes, people get too close. Intrusive and annoying, isn't it? Has he invited you into his apartment recently? Remember, I'll ask him."

"He said he wanted to talk to me about my future. Really, he's just morbid. Fascinated by my downhill slide."

Malc appeared in the doorway before Luke could ask another answer.

"There are two specks of white powder in the toe of one boot."

"Chemical analysis, please."

"Already completed. It is a detergent."

"A detergent?" He glanced at Emily.

She muttered, "I've got to clean them with something."

"What brand of detergent?" Luke asked Malc.

"It was made by Blackwall Detergents but, according

to records, the company has been out of business for six years."

Now there was a pleasant prickling down Luke's spine. He turned towards Emily and said, "Do you have any six-year-old detergent, made in North Greenwich?"

Her long and unsightly face had changed dramatically. It was even more gaunt. She shook her head.

"There's only way you could've picked it up. You've been in the abandoned factory in London. Is that where she is, Emily?"

Chapter Twenty-Four

"You're the FI, not me," Emily retorted. "I'm not even going to make graduation. You figure it out."

"Tell me, and The Authorities will take your cooperation into account."

She stared at him defiantly. "Oh yeah? You're going to charge me with murder. How does my cooperation make any difference to that?"

"It might," Luke replied, knowing that it wouldn't.

Emily changed yet again. A warped smile came to her face. "What are you – and the law – going to do to me? Charge me, put me on trial, find me guilty and give me the death sentence?" She shrugged as if she didn't care. "I won't last that long. Lipodystrophy's already given me a death sentence." She shook her manly head. "You can't touch me. And The Authorities can't touch me. I'm beyond punishment. You've got nothing to bargain with and I've got nothing to lose."

Of course, Luke realized she was right again. The detergent definitely linked her to the abduction in London. Connecting her to EW4 probably connected her to the related Emily Wonders, but not forensically. Luke needed more. But she seemed beaten and willing to talk – perhaps because she had nothing to lose – so he pushed his luck. "Tell me about the contact lens. Did you discover it on your clothes when you got back from Woburn and decide to plant it in Mr Garrett's place, or did you keep it deliberately?"

"When I was scrubbing everything clean, I found it in my coat pocket. I should have destroyed it, but Garrett was getting on my nerves. I knew I could use it to blame him if you began to suspect someone at school."

"The same with the aggregate? When he wasn't looking, you jammed the bits under his shoes, leaving a print behind."

"When you started asking me about family and marine creatures, you got too close for comfort," she admitted. "That's when Garrett became my safety net. I had stones out of my boots and left them, with the lens, in his room. It was easy. He was always offering me tea and biscuits – as if they'd make everything all right, as if they'd cure lipodystrophy. Sometimes it was whole meals. I planted the stuff while he was cooking in the kitchen. I didn't have long but I thought I'd wiped all the prints." She shook her head, clearly annoyed with herself.

"Passing the blame means you didn't want to get caught. You say you're beyond the law but you don't want to go to trial."

She laughed. "Wrong. I was more interested in beating whichever FI they put on the case. I'm not going to reach Final Qualification but I wanted to prove I could've made it. Unfortunately you…" She shook her head again.

"You could've got him executed for murder."

"Am I supposed to be bothered by that? I don't know. Maybe I wouldn't have let it get that far. A deathbed confession would've taken care of it. A dramatic gesture, eh?"

"Those meals he offered you. Did he give you pufferfish?"

"No. But ages ago he told me…" She giggled to herself. "If ever the disease got too much for me, he'd give me something to put me out of my misery. As if I'm the giving-up kind! Anyway, he slipped me a little vial."

Luke nodded. "TTX. Weren't you frightened to handle it?"

"When you're like me – incurable – handling poison loses its fear factor."

He realized that she was opening up because of her illness. The law was powerless to punish someone approaching death, but that was of no concern to an investigator. Luke simply needed to make his case and discover the truth. "But you know I'm going to ask Clint Garrett if he's ever given TTX to anybody and he'll come up with you."

"He won't want to drop me in it, but he will… to save his own skin. Then there's that print. When he thinks about it, he'll say I'm the only one who had the chance to put stones in his shoe and a contact lens in his wardrobe."

"The TTX links you to the Dundee case, the stones to London, and the contact lens to the Woburn murder. You're facing at least three charges."

"Criminal charges lose their fear factor as well when you've got a terminal disease."

"You must have visited the old Emily in York and she told you about her sauna oil. The nurse said she told all her visitors how good it was."

Emily nodded and smiled crookedly. "The silly old fool made it easy. Concentrated almond extract did the rest." She shuffled in her seat. "Anyway, my job's done. There aren't any more Emily Wonders in my family line as far as I can tell."

"There's something I don't understand," he said.

"You're supposed to be the tops," she replied swiftly and spitefully.

"There's plenty of people in your bloodline. Men, women, boys and girls who didn't get lipodystrophy. You've got cause to bear them all a grudge. So why just pick on the ones called Emily?"

"We hatched a plot, me and Emily..."

Taken aback, Luke broke in straightaway. "What? Are you saying your sister was called Emily as well?"

"Yes. You haven't done your research, have you? When she died, my parents tried again and gave me the same name."

"Hang on! She died before you were born?"

"Yes."

"But you said, '*We* hatched a plot.'"

Emily nodded. "It's like she's still with me. A bit like a secret twin. I talk to her all the time. Actually, Emily's more ruthless than me. She wanted me to call on everyone in the family tree and give them a taste of death. If there was a way of injecting them with lipodystrophy, that would've been ideal for her. But it's not like that. It can't be done. And it'd be hundreds of people. I stripped the idea down to Emily Wonders who could've inherited the disease. That's because we're both called Emily." Now, there was moisture in her eyes and her voice was breaking. "You wouldn't believe the research I put into finding them. I've been planning it for years. And I did it. I finished without getting caught. Roll call complete."

Luke shook his head. "No, it isn't. Where's the fourth one?"

She wiped her cheek and looked at the date displayed in the bottom right-hand corner of her telescreen. "They say you can last three minutes without air, three days without water, and three weeks without food. She could still be alive. Just."

"She's locked in the detergent factory, isn't she?"

Stony-faced, she repeated, "You're the FI."

"Yes. It must've been three weeks ago. That fits with my witness. It'd be the Saturday you went to Woburn. December the twenty-fourth. You did your research and, while you were in the south, you tracked the last Emily down in Greenwich that weekend."

"Think you're clever, don't you?"

"Clever enough to get the evidence I need to charge you with the murder of three people called Emily Wonder, abduction and attempted murder of another."

Malc's silence confirmed it.

Luke left her in the hands of the agents and called The Authorities in London straightaway. As soon as he explained that he needed a search and rescue team to comb North Greenwich, his request was denied. The Authorities had channelled all of their resources into dealing with a possible flood because the volcano in the Canary Islands had reached critical status. Luke muttered a curse and flew out of the school, towards the nearest corridor where he dived into a fast cab bound for London.

Without a trace of emotion, Malc roused the dozing Luke with the announcement, "This cab will not be permitted into east London."

Instantly awake, Luke cried, "What? Why not?"

"East London, Thames estuary towns, and all southern coastal communities are being evacuated."

"It's happening, then!"

"The volcano on La Palma has erupted and much of its western side collapsed two hours ago. The resulting wave will flood many southern areas, including low-lying parts of London."

"But the old detergent factory is right by the river."

"Correct."

"I need to talk to The Authorities about Emily Wonder again."

"I have already done so. All personnel are involved in evacuation measures. It is not efficient use of agents and guards to assign them to a search for one person who may already be dead."

"All right. Tell them I'm arriving in this cab. They've got to let me through."

"Denied. Corridor power will be turned off within the danger zone."

"How long have I got?"

"Two hours and thirty-six minutes. It is very unlikely to be enough time to find Emily Wonder and effect a rescue. The Authorities require you to abandon this attempt. It is too dangerous."

"Malc. I am not going to abandon anything. You heard what Edinburgh Emily said. She left EW4 without food for weeks but she could be alive."

"The Authorities do not regard her life as valuable enough to risk yours in these circumstances."

"All human life is precious, Malc. You wouldn't understand."

"Correct. My programming does not call for understanding, only obedience and allegiance to the law."

"Perhaps you'd understand if you faced dying at some point."

"I cannot die, but I will become obsolete one day," Malc said without a hint of regret.

"Enough. Plot me a route to the Thames as near as possible to Greenwich — one that'll stay powered up. Then feed it to the cab. We're going in." He paused before adding, "Then get me a speech-only link to Owen Goode."

Owen's heated voice filled the back of the cab. "It's crazy here. I'm being told to get out."

"It's not some sort of trick, Owen. It's for real. In two and a half hours, a ten-metre wave is going to surge up the river. It'll flood a lot of London."

"No!"

"Yes," Luke insisted. "But ask yourself this. Will The Authorities put much effort into evacuating homeless kids from North Greenwich who probably don't even know what's coming? The warehouse is going to be swamped."

"Right. Got you. I'm on my way. They'll take ages to round up."

"I'll see you there."

"Really? You as well?"

"I think that eleven-year-old's trapped in Blackwall Detergents. I'll take care of her if I can. You get the kids to higher ground. If you can't do it in time, take them to a tower block in Canary Wharf and get up to the top floor."

"I don't have a fancy identity card like yours. I won't be able to get in."

Luke smiled. "Come on! I'm an investigator so I can't tell you to smash a few windows. But the wave'll break far more than you, so don't lose sleep over it. Good luck. You'll need it."

"Yeah. You too," Owen replied in a loud voice, as if he were shouting all the way to Luke's southbound cab. "And thanks."

To the right of the corridor, the clear sky over Derby glowed a glorious red and orange as the sun headed for the horizon. Cocooned within the warm vehicle, Luke did not feel the marked drop in temperature as nightfall neared.

Chapter Twenty-Five

In the North Atlantic Ocean, a ring of mountainous water radiated outwards from the Canary Islands. All shipping in the tsunami's path was steaming away from the area but most would not be able to outrun the rogue wave. They were doomed to be tossed like toys and capsized.

Every telescreen along England's south coast was broadcasting a continuous alert about the coming disaster, urging people to seek out higher ground immediately. Thousands of homes below sea level in Canvey Island and near the Bristol Channel had been forcibly evacuated and abandoned for the duration of the flood. Guards and agents were sweeping across vulnerable parts of London, spreading the message to those who had not heard the telescreen news.

Feeling anxious for an eleven-year-old girl and for himself, Luke could not relax. Yet giving up the bid to rescue Emily had not crossed his mind. Talking online to a voice of The Authorities, he said, "Yes. Twenty or thirty children collect in North Greenwich warehouse and I know you don't have the resources to send agents out to round up people who aren't registered. The kids would scatter even if you did. But I'm saying I could get Owen Goode to rescue them all. That means you wash your hands of them. Afterwards, you won't have to justify not attempting to save them. Even if it's terrible news, you can say you sent someone in to do his best. It's the same with me and the trapped girl."

"You're stepping well beyond your sphere of expertise, Investigator Harding."

"I know. But it makes sense."

"What does this Owen Goode want in return?"

"Not a lot. Just the dome – if it's still standing after the wave. And the freedom to run a sort of sanctuary there. He'll lure a good few kids away from crime."

Astounding Luke, Malc added, "I confirm it is a logical course of action. Owen Goode is skilled at organizing and restraining such children."

Luke stared at his mobile and then nodded his thanks for the unexpected support. "I might even be able to persuade Jed Lester – the runner – to help out."

It was fully ninety seconds before Luke got a reply. "We have agreed. If Owen Goode is successful at saving the children, he will be allowed to use the warehouse as a youth shelter, subject to our inspections."

Luke was glad he was not on telescreen because he could not resist punching the air in triumph and grinning widely. "Thank you," he replied, as soberly as possible. "I will contact him and see if he is willing to risk... you know."

Malc severed the link to The Authorities and said, "I

remind you that you have already gained Owen Goode's cooperation."

Luke nodded. "But it's not always the best policy to reveal your hand. I mean, to do things the proper way round."

The cab continued its frantic dash towards the Thames. Luke and Malc seemed to be the only ones going against the tide of people. Entering the outskirts of the ugly city at nightfall, the corridor lamps held back darkness. The cab swung round corners at speed, searching out intact and passable freeways, until it came to a halt at Chelsea Bridge to the west of Central London. On the opposite bank, Battersea geothermal power station was deserted and out of order. Its dark silhouette was eerily silent. Under artificial lighting, workers at Battersea Green Animal Sanctuary were sandbagging the perimeter as a precaution.

"When the surge reaches this far inland," Malc told him, "it will have diminished to levels that should not be dangerous."

Luke wasted no time. He sprinted to the wharf, asking, "How far is it up the river to Blackwall Detergents?"

"Sixteen point three kilometres," Malc answered.

Luke swiped his card through the quayside reader and said, "Urgent. North Greenwich. Fastest transport available."

The auto-system was still working. The computer-generated voice replied, "Pier 3."

Luke squinted through the gloom. Pier 7 was in front of him and Pier 8 was to his right. He dashed to the left and zigzagged through the complex of landing stages. Attached to Pier 3 was a powerboat. "Fantastic," Luke said as he clambered on board, guided by a single lamp above the stage. "Never been on one, but it looks fast."

The attachments disengaged and the engine let out an unearthly clatter. Luke staggered back as the launch lurched and accelerated quickly to maximum.

Shouting above the noise, Luke said, "Calculate our speed. How long will I have in North Greenwich before the flood comes?"

The boat turned northwards, powered past Thomas's Hospital, and headed for Central London. Two red lights at the stern acted as a warning. A single white light on the prow illuminated the river in front. The water heaved gently like the chest of a sleeping giant. There was no clue that the giant would soon wake and cause havoc.

"At this rate," Malc replied, "you will have thirty-seven minutes to reach safety."

They were charging directly towards the massive wave that would gush through London. As far as Luke could see as he clung to the powerboat rail, the centre of the city was deserted. The river turned eastwards and the launch raced between the ruins of Southwark

Bridge, under London Bridge and then passed Tower Bridge. Moonlight and the river walkway lamps picked out a foaming white wake behind the craft. Standing near the bow, Luke seemed to be the only person on the Thames.

The powerboat rocked as it swung past Rotherhithe and Luke gripped the wet rail tighter. He waited for the launch to swerve violently in the other direction when it took the big bend by the tower blocks of Canary Wharf. Water sprayed out from under the prow and the wind blew Luke's damp hair in all directions. The boat was travelling south now, through a barren landscape that had become familiar to him. The engine's tone changed. It was powering down, ready to sweep round the tight curve and head north to the Greenwich warehouse. It was only a matter of minutes before Luke would be on dry land, making a dash from the wharf to the detergent factory.

Even before the attachments locked the launch to the platform alongside a river cruiser, Luke leapt onto the jetty, skidding on the slushy snow. Without faltering, he sprinted towards the entrance to Blackwall Tunnel and the dome. Malc shone a light over his shoulder onto the decaying freeway.

Ahead, Owen Goode was leading a band of scruffy kids away from the area. When Owen saw Luke charging towards him, he turned to them and calmed them down. "It's all right. Don't be frightened! He's an FI but he's here to help. Promise. Stay together."

At Owen's side, the seven-year-old agreed. "He's okay, this one."

Reassured, the children did not panic and flee.

Luke paused. "Have you got your identity card?" Seeing Owen nod, he said, "Good. Go down to the quay and ask for Canary Wharf. You've got half an hour. A bit more. You'll make it into a tower block."

"What about you?"

"I can look after myself."

Owen smiled. "Oh yeah? Only because of him." He jerked a thumb towards Malc.

Luke slapped Owen on the back. "Good news. If the warehouse is still in one piece in the morning, it's yours. You've got yourself your own youth centre." Then he ran off into the night.

Behind Luke, Owen's open-mouthed expression of surprise evolved into a broad grin.

At the disintegrating wooden gate, Luke stopped and took some deep breaths. "Right. Let's go round it, looking for signs someone's broken in."

The first obstacle was the padlock on the gate. Luke lifted his boot and slammed it into the wood. There was the sound of tearing but it did not splinter completely. The second attempt loosened it even further. Luke did not want to drain Malc's batteries unless he had to, so he did not ask the mobile to fire his laser. Instead, he kicked again and the gate fell limply to one side. Squeezing through the gap into the concrete yard, Luke saw a large pile of caked white powder. It looked like a snowdrift but it was made of unused detergent.

He dashed to the main door and Malc shone a light onto it. It was filthy, apparently undisturbed for years.

"There are no indications that it has been opened and no footprints in the dirt," Malc told him.

Luke began to circle the old building, stopping by each window and testing it for movement and traces of entry. When he bashed his fist against the rear fire door, he sent a hollow boom throughout the empty structure. "Still nothing?" he asked Malc.

"I do not detect any evidence of recent interference."

Luke could not see a ladder or anything else that would have given access the upper floor but he got Malc to scan the higher windows anyway.

Once he'd completed a circuit of the factory, he came to a halt. His sigh became visible in the chilly air. "I was sure she'd…" He shook his head. "How long have we got?"

"Twenty-three minutes and forty-two seconds."

Frustrated, Luke closed his eyes for a few moments. "This isn't right. That young lad said the two Emilys walked off that way," he said, pointing east, beyond the dome. "Towards the river. Why?"

"It is likely that the business shipped its product by auto-barge," Malc remarked.

"Brilliant! There'll be a terminal somewhere. I bet that's it."

Chapter Twenty-Six

Luke set off at speed again. He stopped at the spot where he'd first caught sight of Emily's blue backpack. The waterfront lamps were struggling to make an impression on the darkness and Luke relied on Malc to act as a beacon. His fingers grasped the rusty rail but he let go at once because it felt freezing against his skin.

"There!" Luke shouted, pointing northwards. He'd spotted the jetty that floated at a crazy angle. Once, a long time ago, it had provided a mooring for auto-barges. He imagined that the silo fed detergent into their holds. "Let's go."

He sprinted along the walkway until he reached the point where the floating stage was fastened. There, his heart fell. On the bank, there was a padlocked iron gate to bar the way onto the rickety wooden plank, held up by corroded scaffolding.

Malc surveyed it and said, "This construction will not withstand the force of a ten-metre surge." Then he homed in on the ironwork and added, "The gate has been forced open and fitted with a new padlock. There are scrape marks in the rust where an object like a crowbar was levered. On the plank, there is evidence of footprints…"

Luke couldn't wait for Malc to burn through iron

with his laser. "Give me light," he ordered, intent on clambering around the gate to get onto the boards that sloped down to the pontoon. He grasped a metal pole on the right-hand side of the gate and tested its strength. It was very cold to the touch but at least the pitted rusty surface gave him a good grip. The ground below his feet dropped away as he swung out, taking his weight on his arms. Dangling from the scaffolding, he inched out over the river by shuffling his hands along the girder. When he'd got past the gate, he pulled himself up acrobatically and rolled onto the plank.

As he got to his feet, the wood creaked and flexed alarmingly. But he didn't have time to worry about his own safety or the sturdiness of the contraption. He strode onto the ramshackle jetty itself. He couldn't walk easily on its surface because it was nowhere near flat. Crossing it was like teetering on a steep hillside. It also wobbled with the river's movement. There were three heavy metal covers that protected storage chambers below the waterline. First, though, Luke pointed to the silo. "Am I right, Malc? Are there any detergent residues around it?"

"Confirmed."

Luke sighed with relief. "Okay, let's see if one of these chambers has been disturbed."

This time, he didn't need Malc's sophisticated scanning. He needed only the mobile's spotlight.

"Here!"

The dirt around the middle lid had been removed and there were scratches on the metal. Again, there was a fresh padlock keeping it firmly in place. "I want this open." But Luke could not see any tools lying on the frail landing stage so he had no choice but to use his mobile. "Zap it, Malc. Find the weakest point and burn right through."

To conserve power, Malc turned off his light and channelled all of his energy into the laser. The padlock was the obvious target but it was new and tough. Instead, he focussed on the old bolt that secured the U-shaped staple to the platform.

In the darkness, the intense narrow beam glowed red and bright. Luke looked away because it stung his eyes. "I bet this is where Emily's rucksack toppled into the Thames, you know."

"Insufficient data."

"How long have I got?"

"Fifteen minutes and…"

"All right. That'll do. Get through it as quickly as you can."

A tower crane loomed over Luke as he sat on the uneven surface, clutching a heavy iron ring that had been concreted into place. Years ago, barges had been tied to it, but now Luke used it to make sure he didn't slide off the jetty and into the Thames.

He was only centimetres above the softly lapping water. If he didn't move in the next quarter of an hour, he'd feel the full, lethal effect of a ten-metre wave. Right now, the river was tranquil, giving no hint of the mayhem to come. It was hard to believe that anything catastrophic was about to happen on such a still night. It was so quiet that it was creepy. People were not the only inhabitants who had fled. Instinct had driven away the animals and birds.

Breaking the silence, Luke banged on the lid and shouted, "Emily!"

There was no response. He suspected that noise would not penetrate the bulky cover.

"Come on, Malc," he said. "Hurry up."

The robot turned off his laser and shone a light onto the landing stage. "I suggest you try a sharp impact."

Luke scrambled to his feet and kicked the staple as hard as he could. "Ow!"

The fixing remained in place.

Ignoring the pain in his toes, Luke lashed out a second time. "No good."

Malc moved to a new position and activated the laser again, tackling the lock from a different angle.

Fidgeting, Luke stood and shivered. Clasping his hands together was not keeping them warm so he shoved them into his coat pockets. Nursing his foot, he waited until he was required to kick again.

The bolt let out a twang and Malc killed the laser.

At once, Luke rammed his foot into the fastening and the padlock flew like a football into the river with a splash. Dropping to his knees, Luke grabbed the handle.

"Beware. It will be hot..."

Paying no attention, Luke yanked on the cover. At first it hardly budged. Realizing that it was very heavy, Luke put one foot either side, leaned down and pulled with all of his strength. The lid came up, revealing a damp detergent store and an eleven-year-old girl lying like an unwanted doll flat out on top of a mouldy heap of powder.

Luke knelt down and thrust both arms towards her. "She's warm," he said. He got a hand under each of her arms, steadied himself, and then lifted her out into the chilly night air. She remained unconscious.

"As a matter of utmost urgency," Malc told him, "you must reach firm and higher ground."

It was then, just as he was about to celebrate, that his true predicament struck him. Looking around, he realized he was a long way from anywhere secure. He could not even get Emily off the platform because of the padlocked gate.

"Can you call a boat remotely, Malc?"

"Confirmed."

"Go on, then. Get that fast launch."

After a few seconds, Malc replied, "It was taken by

Owen Goode. A cruiser is coming from the wharf."

"How long before the wave gets here?"

"Seven minutes exactly."

"There's only the warehouse and I can't make it in time."

"That is incorrect," Malc said. "I calculated your running speed while you were interviewing Jed Lester. At that speed you could sprint to it and climb one of the external ladders to a safe height on its roof if you were not burdened with Emily Wonder. There is no ground or stable building of the required height within seven minutes if you carry her."

"So, I dump her here. She drowns and I save myself?"

"That is one option."

"No it isn't," Luke uttered angrily. "If I drape her over you, could you lift her up?"

"No. I am not designed for heavy lifting. I do not have the required power."

Luke looked downstream. "Where's that boat?"

"Coming."

"I can't beat the wave upriver in it, can I?"

"No."

Luke had exhausted his options and his hope. He had found Emily alive and rescued her only so that they could die together in the coming frenzy of the Thames.

Whenever Luke felt discouraged, he drew comfort

from looking at the stars. This hushed night, the sky was clear and vast, and the light from the nearest stars was beautifully bright. He sighed and swivelled to take it all in for the last time. But it was not just a favourite formation that caught his eye.

"The crane, Malc! Will the wave knock it over?"

"I cannot answer without a structural survey and information on the weight of its various parts."

"What's your best guess? I mean, your best estimate? Quickly."

The mobile was silent for a few precious seconds. "It is possible that it will withstand the surge. It is positioned very close to a brick wall. If the crane tilts, the wall will prop it up if the bricks resist the force of the waves."

At last, the cruiser came into view and pulled alongside the sloping pontoon. Luke lifted Emily in both arms and dropped her into the boat, then he jumped in himself. Instead of asking Malc to give a destination, he grabbed hold of the landing stage and heaved until the boat moved towards the bank. He tugged again and again until the jetty was out of his reach and the cruiser was drifting gently to the shore.

Seeing a length of rope lying in the bottom of the boat, Luke grabbed it and tied Emily's wrists together as quickly as his cold fingers could manage. Picking her up again, he plonked her down on the mud and then scrambled out onto the land himself. Looping her arms over his head so her joined hands fell across his chest, he lifted her up on his back and scrambled up the bank onto the walkway.

Trying to raise his own spirits as he made for the crane, he said, "Luckily, I am designed for heavy lifting. Pomegranates make you big and strong, you know."

"The nutritional content…"

"Stop," Luke cried. "Just light my way."

Wearing Emily like a bulky and cumbersome backpack, Luke climbed up the steps to the crane's neglected cabin, full of levers, pedals, knobs and dials jammed into position by corrosion. He did not attempt to get into the cubicle through the door or a smashed window because he knew it wasn't high enough above the Thames.

"You are currently four point one metres above river level," Malc informed him, "and I estimate that the main wave will reach this position in three minutes and eleven seconds."

Daunted, Luke looked skywards. A long and rusty ladder in the crane's neck led up to another control box, nestling just below the enormous horizontal arm. It was so far above him that he thought he might as well reach for the stars. But he had no choice. He had to put another six metres between him and the ground. At least six metres. Standing on top of the cabin, he grasped the frozen ladder. As soon as he planted his foot on the first rung, he realized that it was slippery with ice. Cursing, he had to make sure that, every time he took a step up, he pressed the heel of his boot against the rung so that he did not slip off. He tried not to look up to the jib and winch overhead, or down to the ground. Instead, he gazed eastwards across Greenwich, towards Woolwich and Bexley but he didn't take in anything other than a string of glowing dots like little stars along the twists of the Thames. He tried to ignore the limp girl on his back and simply concentrate on where he placed his hands and feet. At least Emily was light after three weeks without food. Slowly, he pulled himself up and up.

"Warning," Malc said, hovering to his side. "The next rung is dangerously corroded."

Luke was too tired to reply. He took a deep breath and lifted his right leg higher, missing out the next step. But his awkward movement made him slip and Emily shifted. Her tied hands closed around his neck and the rope began to choke him, making it impossible to swallow and breathe.

Malc flew behind him and pushed against Emily's backside, supporting her body as much as possible.

Luke regained his footholds and clung to the ladder firmly with one fist. With the other, he pulled the rope and her hands away from his throat.

An icy wind was whistling through the framework. Luke's fingers were nearly numb. His toes and lungs ached with the cold and his shoulders throbbed with the strain of taking Emily's weight.

Returning to Luke's side, Malc said, "I am programmed to protect you. If that happens again, threatening your life, I will burn through the rope and release the girl."

Luke was too exhausted to argue. He continued to climb. Daring to look down, he guessed that he was about the height of four men from the cabin.

Sensing a rumbling noise above the screeching of the wind, he glanced along the path of the squirming river. A heart-stopping wall of water came into his view. As it hurtled towards him, it knocked out the waterfront lamps in a series of mini-explosions. The arch of water swept through and over the Thames barrier as if it weren't there. Soon, the rumble became a terrifying roar, like the sound of a thousand waterfalls.

"Malc!" Luke screamed. "Am I high enough?"

"Confirm..."

His mobile's flat voice was lost in the din.

The giant wave crashed into the crane, about a metre below Luke's feet. At once, the whole contraption began to tilt and rotate. Above him, the giant jib twisted and the winch fell heavily down into the raging water.

Luke's left foot slid off the slippery rung. He grasped

tighter with his unfeeling hands and pushed the heel of his right boot harder against the tread so it dug into the arch of his foot. He hung on for his life.

Battered by the surging water, the framework leaned more and more. Malc manoeuvred himself against the crane's upright in an attempt to halt its slump towards the water but his effort was useless. It was like asking a sandcastle to hold back the incoming tide.

Clinging to the iron network, Luke braced himself.

Chapter Twenty-Seven

The long neck of the crane juddered and jarred, then ceased its tilt. Luke swore and gripped even tighter as the jolt threatened to nudge him from the machinery. He looked down but all he could see below him was swirling floodwater. Somewhere underneath, the crane must have come to rest against the brick wall. Now, his fate also rested on the wall. If it collapsed under the pressure of water, he would be plunged with Emily into the torrent. If it resisted the deluge, he could yet save her and himself.

Beneath his feet, the rung jerked again as the crane settled. Maybe it had dislodged some bricks, making itself snug against the wall. Maybe, if more bricks collapsed, he'd be pitched into the flood. But, a minute later, there was no further movement and Luke began to breathe more easily.

Malc no longer illuminated the scene. He was swaying in the air, unable to compensate for the gusting wind. He moved to a position above Luke's head and wedged himself in the lattice of the crane's ironwork. "Stay where you are," he said to Luke. "There will be waves for several minutes. They will not be as large as the leading tsunami. My power level requires me to shut down in twenty-eight seconds."

"Thanks, Malc," Luke gasped. "One last job for you. Put out an emergency call to The Authorities. I need a rescue boat and a medical team as soon as they can sort it out."

"Transmitting."

Luke smiled at him and said, "That's right. You have a good sleep while I do all the work."

"I do not..." Malc's mechanical voice stuttered and stopped.

A new dread enveloped Luke. He was alone and defenceless. Above him, his mobile was drained of power. Attached to his back, Emily was also lifeless. He was stuck up an unstable crane and below him London was awash and deserted. The water level had fallen but great swells still came and went. Where there had been builders' yards and corridors, there was now a rippling sea. Only the rounded roof of the warehouse poked out of the water. The wave must have filled Blackwall Tunnel and swept away the other wrecked buildings of North Greenwich.

Speaking to no one, he said, "At least the warehouse is still there. Owen's got a job – if he's any good at water polo."

Strangely, once Luke got used to the crane's tilted position, it was easier for him to bear Emily's weight. Instead of being upright and supporting her on his shoulders, he was stretched across the framework of poles and she was lying across his back. Of course, he had no way of knowing if she was still alive.

He lay there for ten minutes, watching waves come and go like aftershocks of the tsunami. Once the water had receded so that he could see the top of the crane's cabin again, he struggled down the ladder slowly, painfully and carefully.

It was difficult to stand on the roof of the control box because it was on such a slant. With a filthy pool below him, it reminded him of the dilapidated landing stage. He lowered Emily so that she was propped between the roof and the wall that had saved their lives. If she was breathing, it was too shallow and weak for him to detect. His fingers were deadened with cold and strain but he was sure that he could feel a pulse in her neck. He stripped off his fleece and wrapped it around her motionless body. Then, exhausted and marooned, he sat with his back against the bricks and waited for The Authorities to rescue him.

The icy spell came to an end ten days later. Seen from his hotel window, the hills at the edge of the Peak District had become green and brown again. Luke could also make out the silvery top of the geothermal power station. He stood with his hands on the windowsill and Jade's arms around his waist. Bliss. And a lot less strenuous than having an unconscious Emily Wonder draped around him.

Malc broke into the moment to announce, "You have a request for a connection from Owen Goode."

Jade stepped to one side and Luke pointed at the wall that held a telescreen. "On there."

Straightaway, it was plain that Owen was on a high. "You'll never guess who turned up at the warehouse!"

"I won't bother trying then," Luke replied, using logic that Malc would have been proud of.

"Jed Lester!"

Luke smiled, pretending to be surprised. "*The* Jed Lester, or someone else with the same name?"

"The runner. You know. Likely, he's going to get an indoor running track put in, if he can twist a few arms."

"That's great," Luke said. "Amazing how word gets around when you take on a good cause." Luke glanced across the room and then said, "I'll see if I can organize a top musician to come down and give you a performance."

Owen pulled a face. "Emily Wonder? My kids won't be into that sort of thing."

Luke laughed at the thought. "No. More nightclub gig than opera."

"That's better." Owen hesitated and then asked, "Who's that? Someone with weird hair – red and blond – just went behind you."

"She's the musician for your party performance. Jade."

"She looked all right."

Luke nodded. "Mmm. She is."

"Good for you," Owen replied with a grin.

Luke didn't want to bring him down. Even so, he could not resist saying, "But pairing's a different matter."

"Ah. You want to talk to The Authorities about that. While you're at it, remember to put in a word for Everton Kohter. Two and a bit weeks to go before the death penalty, I think." Distracted, Owen turned away for a moment and then said, "Talking of Emily Wonder, there's someone here wants a word."

"Oh?"

When Owen stood back awkwardly, still not used to telescreens, a small plump girl appeared in front of him. Luke hardly recognized her. Last time he'd seen Greenwich Emily, she was as thin as a stick and seriously ill. In Thomas's Hospital, she'd told him that a tall and strange-looking young woman had asked for her help with someone she'd just dragged from the Thames. Of course, the drowned person hadn't existed. Emily remembered being hit from behind and left on the jetty in a cramped container. Luke had shown her a picture of Edinburgh Emily Wonder and, before the exhausted patient had closed her eyes again, she'd identified her would-be murderer.

"Hello," she said, glancing at Luke through the telescreen but then, embarrassed, she looked down.

A healthy tan colour had returned to her face. "You look fantastic. How are you doing?"

"Good now. I had someone from… you know… The Authorities visit me in hospital. Told me what you did."

"They probably exaggerated," Luke said. "Anyway, you did better yourself, surviving on the water that trickled in. Very brave."

"I just wanted to say thank you."

"No problem."

"The girl who attacked me. Is she… you know?"

"It's okay. You're safe," Luke said. "She's under guard in Edinburgh Hospital. The doctors tell me she's got less than a month to live."

"Just like she gave me."

Luke nodded and then changed the subject. "How do you like the warehouse?"

"Great," she answered, her face beaming now. "Still wet and bashed about, but we're fixing it up."

"Just promise me one thing."

"What's that?"

"You won't start singing opera."

Emily Wonder looked surprised for a moment and then, realizing that even an FI wasn't serious all of the time, she giggled. "No chance. I've gone off boats and swimming as well."

Want to find out about Luke Harding's next exciting case? Here is the first chapter of the next Traces *story,* Double Check. *Read on for a taste of more forensic crime-solving with Luke and Malc.*

TRACES: DOUBLE CHECK

A shiver enveloped the official executioner's body when he stepped into the empty Death Cell. He always reacted badly to the dreadful atmosphere as he entered the cold chamber in Block J of Cambridge Prison. Greg didn't let the unpleasant prickling put him off, though. To distract himself, he thought about how he'd been selected for this job. He was certain that he'd been chosen from all of the prison guards because his name, Greg Roper, sounded most like the Grim Reaper. That brought an ironic smile to his lips.

There were no windows and only two pieces of furniture in the small room: a bed that could be tilted from almost upright to horizontal and a wooden cabinet on wheels. First, Greg opened the cabinet and checked that the chemicals were all present and correct. Sodium pentothal would put the prisoner to sleep. Pancuronium bromide would paralyse his lungs and diaphragm, then potassium chloride would stop his heart. The whole process of delivering the death sentence was designed to take between fifteen and twenty minutes. Greg was proud of his record: thirteen and a half minutes from strapping of the inmate onto the bed to the ending of life. After all, he didn't want to prolong the suffering of anyone, even a murderer.

He checked that there was enough saline solution to wash the tubes that would deliver the fatal sequence of chemicals. He measured the tubes to make sure that they were long enough and then he inspected both intravenous needles. One would be placed in the criminal's arm and the other was a spare in case something went wrong. Not that the procedure had ever gone wrong in Greg's hands.

Satisfied, he turned his attention to the bed and said to the computer, "Upright position, please." Greg whispered really. He always whispered in the Death Cell. With its belts and fastenings dangling grimly, the bed tipped slowly until it was almost vertical. It came to a halt without a hint of shuddering. Everything had to be perfect. Perfectly smooth was how Greg liked it. That's why he practised, checked and double-checked well before an execution. "Project a life-size hologram of Everton Kohter onto it, please."

The image didn't look totally like the real thing. It was a mere ghost of a man. Or boy in this case. In nineteen days, Everton would become the smallest, youngest person that Greg had ever strapped onto the bed. He knelt down and made sure that the lower ties were correctly adjusted to attach to the prisoner's ankles. He didn't want to have to fiddle with the buckles while the poor boy waited to die. The long belts that would encircle his waist and chest seemed fine. At the top of the bed, the forehead loop needed to be five millimetres shorter to stop Everton jerking his head. Greg wanted it tight so that the prisoner could not possibly damage himself if he struggled.

Finally, Greg ensured that the arm restraints were functioning properly and set for Everton's measurements. Once the intravenous needle was in place under his skin, it was vital that the prisoner could not free an arm from the strap and thrash around. That way, he could dislodge the delivery tube.

Content, Greg said in a hushed voice, "That's all. End programme."

The virtual version of Everton Kohter disappeared at once. When the real thing had been put to sleep and the prison doctor had pronounced bleakly, "Life extinct," Greg would call in two of his colleagues to take the body away. And hopefully he would be able to congratulate himself on an efficient job well done.

It was no use telling The Authorities that he was alone in his hotel room. Luke knew that Jade would keep very quiet, he was sure he could lie confidently and persuasively, but he was equally certain that his mobile aid to law and crime would correct any fib. "Er… No. I have Jade Vernon with me," he said.

"I see." The words spoken by Malc were not delivered in the usual male monotone. The female voice emerging from him carried an element of opinion and it sounded to Luke like disapproval. "Never mind. Your mobile tells us you're in Sheffield. This is convenient."

"Oh?"

The Authorities had hijacked the mobile robot's synthetic speech circuitry to talk to Luke. "We are assigning you to a case of possible corruption there. It has come to our attention that some people in Sheffield may have been paired inappropriately and unconventionally."

Puzzled, Luke frowned and glanced at the silent Jade.

"At least one member of the local Pairing Committee may have been unduly influenced."

Luke could not resist interrupting. "Influenced? What does that mean?"

At once, Malc's neutral male voice returned for a few seconds. "Persuaded, often by secret or unfair use of wealth or position; affected or altered by indirect or subtle means; swayed to modify the condition, development or outcome of something."

"Thanks, Malc," Luke muttered sarcastically. "Everything's a lot clearer now."

The voice of the Authorities continued, "It's up to

you to find out what form the influence takes, whether a committee member has succumbed to such pressure and, if so, who it is. If it's more than one member, it's your job to find out how many are involved and to identify them."

"But…"

"What?"

Luke could not admit to his doubts. He hated pairing committees. After all, they stood between him and a lifetime paired with Jade. If there was a way around the system of making life partners, he would rather celebrate than investigate it. But he was an FI. It was his duty to uphold the law. He could not pick and choose the rules he'd enforce. "I… um… I've only ever taken on murder cases."

"And you've done exceptionally well. This investigation is easier and lower profile. Think of it as a reward. After all," she added, "a change is as good as a rest." Her attempt at friendliness and informality came across as sinister.

"Do I have a choice?" Luke asked as he gazed into Jade's disbelieving face.

"No. Being in Sheffield, you're ideal for the job."

Luke sighed. "You'll download all relevant notes to Malc?"

"Of course."

"There's something else," Luke said nervously.

"What's that?" the voice of The Authorities asked, clearly irritated that Luke dared to bring up another matter.

"It's... er... the case of Everton Kohter. He's scheduled for execution in two or three weeks. I want to look into it. You know. Just to make sure."

"Is this a serious request, FI Harding?"

"Yes."

"We do not raise doubts in the law without a very good reason."

"The good reason is, you could kill someone who's not done anything wrong. He was supposed to have murdered someone two years back. But mobiles have improved a lot since then. There's no harm in checking he's guilty with up-to-date methods."

There were a few moments of hesitation. "There is harm. It lies in reducing confidence in the law. Besides, I have now got the Kohter file on my monitor. The case against him is utterly watertight. He was arrested within minutes. I'd go as far as to say no one's ever been more clearly guilty of murder."

Deciding not to cave in, Luke swallowed. "There's no problem getting a second opinion, then. I'll agree, and Kohter will be put to death knowing everything's been double-checked."

Malc's speech centre fell silent for a minute. Then the female voice sounded again. "We have granted your request. Reluctantly. I'll download all case notes to your mobile."

"Thanks," Luke replied. "Can you give him holographic programming, as well? I'll want him to recreate the crime scene so I can take a virtual walk though it and get a good look."

"Agreed, but I promise you won't have to be thorough to verify this verdict. And you won't need long but, for obvious reasons, you have nineteen days – until dawn on Sunday the twelfth of February. Kohter's execution will not be delayed."

The link to The Authorities broken, Jade stared at Luke. It wasn't often that she was lost for words. It wasn't for long either. "Inappropriate pairing?" she exclaimed. "Was that for real?"

"Sounds like it's my job to find out."

"Huh. There's more going on than that. They know about you and me." She nodded towards the robot that hovered beside Luke. "Malc tells them. He's probably telling them what we're saying now."

"Incorrect. Your current conversation is not relevant to either investigation."

"It might be in a second," Jade retorted. "They know we'd jump at the chance of inappropriate and unconventional pairing, so why give you the case?"

Not wanting to reveal his fears, Luke shrugged.

It was Malc who put Luke's suspicions into words.

"Your loyalty to the law may be under test."

Luke looked at his mobile. "Do you know that? Have you been told that's what's going on?"

"No. It is a matter of logical deduction. Another explanation is that you are available and suitably located."

Luke smiled wryly. He expected that his mobile's obligation to the law, to the truth, and to himself would also come under test, and into conflict, before he got to the bottom of any illicit pairing. What concerned him more, though, was the looming execution of Everton Kohter…